THE MAN FROM SOCORRO

When Major da Souza killed Abe
Jackson and wounded his brother,
he never guessed at the fateful
outcome. Waylaid and bushwacked
and his own brother shot dead
by the remaining Jackson brothers,
Luke da Souza is found and
cared for by John Lacey and his
daughter, Marie-Anne. Five years
later, when danger and death come
to Sweetwater Valley, they remember
Luke's promising help whenever it
is needed. So they send for the man
from Socorro, and that was when
the lead really began to fly.

Books by Curt Longbow
in the Linford Western Library:

THE LAND GRABBERS

CURT LONGBOW

THE MAN FROM SOCORRO

Complete and Unabridged

LINFORD
Leicester

First published in Great Britain in 1998 by
Robert Hale Limited
London

First Linford Edition
published 1999
by arrangement with
Robert Hale Limited
London

British Library CIP Data

Longbow, Curt
    The man from Socorro.—Large print ed.—
Linford western library
    1. Western stories
    2. Large type books
    I. Title
    823.9'14 [F]

    ISBN 0–7089–5539–8

Published by
F. A. Thorpe (Publishing) Ltd.
Anstey, Leicestershire

Set by Words & Graphics Ltd.
Anstey, Leicestershire
Printed and bound in Great Britain by
T. J. International Ltd., Padstow, Cornwall

Prologue

John Lacey finished his drink and put the empty glass on the bar, then wiped his lips on his sleeve.

'I'll be off now, Sam. See you next month, God willing.'

'So soon, John? What's your hurry? Got a fire up your backside?'

'Nope! I've got Marie-Anne with me and I want to get back before dark. Brought her in as a treat. I keep forgetting she's nearly fourteen and is beginning to want a woman's fal-de-lals. I left her at the store; then she was going to spend some time at the schoolhouse with her old friends and Miss Bentley. I got to pick her up there.'

'Still has her head in Miss Bentley's books then?'

'Aye, that she has. A bright little miss is Marie-Anne. The schoolmarm says

1

she would have made a good teacher, given the chance.'

Sam shook his head and sucked air through his teeth.

'Now that would be a mistake, John. A regular hoity-toity female that one. No wonder she never found a husband! She'd make your kid hoity-toity too, besides keeping her head in a book instead of milking the cows and making butter!'

'Oh, Marie-Anne's not like that. She does her chores right willing, now her ma is gone. She only reads when she's done for the day, and she's useful to me when I want a letter writ.'

'Well, you know best, John, but I never believed in spoiling good wenches. Keep 'em in their place, says I, and you get no trouble.'

'Well, we all have different ways of looking at things. Anyhow, I'll get along. See you next month and maybe we can get a card school going, eh?'

'That would be right nice, John. I'll see you then.' Sam plunged John's glass into a tub of dirty water and rinsed and dried it with a grey-looking towel. He shook his head. A regular good guy, no trouble even when he'd had a drink too many. A pity he let that kid of his wrap him round her finger. Marie-Anne sure was the apple of his eye.

John Lacey let the batwings swing behind him and stepped off the boardwalk to go and hitch up his wagon which now held an assortment of dry goods from the store and some mysterious packages that would be Marie-Anne's, a couple of spades, a kettle and a newfangled washboard the lass had set her heart on.

He looked up as he made the load secure and saw Amos Jackson coming towards him. He raised a hand in greeting.

'Amos! It's been a long time! How's things with you?' Amos owned the biggest ranch in the valley on the other side of the Snake River. Most of the land at that side belonged to him. On this side, the land was divided into three small ranches, of which one was John's.

'Not good, John. Haven't you heard? I lost Abe at Petersburg and young Ned lost an arm.'

'Hell, Amos, I'm sorry. I didn't know!'

'You want to thank God you never had a son! They were accused of desertion during the battle and it was one of our officers who shot 'em! I'll get the bastard if it's the last thing I do!'

'When did it happen, Amos?'

'Two weeks ago, just before the surrender. Mark and Hank are out there stalking him now. If they don't get him, I will. Nobody hurts my family and gets away with it!'

John Lacey saw the hint of madness born of grief in the staring eyes. Abe had been the eldest and wildest of Amos's sons and, to him, the sun had always shone out of the boy's backside. John shook his head.

'I'm sure sorry, Amos. Who was the

4

bastard who shot them?'

'Name of Luke da Souza, from down near the Rio Grande. Joined the Rebs because his mother came from New Orleans and her folk kept slaves.'

'A pity your boys joined up. They should have stayed at home.'

Amos Jackson sighed. 'You know what Abe was like, wild and untamed. Never wanted to be thought a coward and, of course, the other boys went along, too. They thought it would be a great adventure. They didn't think of me managing the ranch with just a few cowhands.' He sighed again. 'I'm getting old, John, and now they're home it means rounding up a lot of wild steers left to theirselves during the war years, and starting again. It'll not be the same without Abe. Hell! I need a drink!' He slammed past John and made for the saloon.

John shook his head as he climbed up on the buckboard and slapped the reins as the horses moved forward. It was sure hard on old Jackson. He'd aged ten years since he'd seen him last.

Marie-Anne was waiting when he arrived at the schoolhouse. In her arms was a stack of books and Miss Bentley was standing beside her to wave her off. Marie-Anne was one of her favourite one-time pupils and she'd wished the girl could stay on longer, but when her ma died she was needed at home. It was a pity. She acknowledged John Lacey's greeting and waved as they moved off. She would miss the girl's lively chatter. She hoped the humdrum life on the ranch wouldn't crush the bright spark that was her spirit.

The two horses were fresh and they made good time along the winding dusty road. The buckboard swayed and bucked as it bounced over bumps and ruts, the horses keen to get home to their own corral. Marie-Anne clung to the side with one hand and clutched her bonnet with the other. Her backside was bruised and her back ached. It was an uncomfortable ride, but worth it to have a day with Miss Bentley and hear the town gossip from Polly Thwaites and Ellen Beechcroft. She wasn't sure she believed Ellen when she said she had a beau, but then Ellen was a whole year older. Maybe she was telling the truth after all.

She was so busy trying to figure out who the beau might be because Ellen had gone all coy and wouldn't disclose his name, that she failed to notice why her father was pulling up the horses and hauling on the brake in a hurry.

'What is it, Pa?'

John pointed with his whip at a stand of trees some distance from the road. Two saddled horses were quietly grazing in the shadows. There was no one to be seen.

'You stay here, Marie-Anne, while I go take a look. They look like army horses to me and, if they are, they're trained to stand and wait.'

He got down stiffly from the wagon and stumped across the rough parched earth and Marie-Anne was quick to see he'd drawn his trusty old gun as a precautionary measure.

She saw him pause and look down and then squat on his heels not far from the horses. Then he stood up and waved to her. He shouted in a stentorian bellow, 'Bring the wagon over here. There's a wounded man and we'll have to get him aboard!'

Slowly and carefully she drove off the dirt road and on to the rough terrain and came to a stop beside her father. It was then she saw the dead body lying beside the wounded man.

They both wore the dirty ragged uniforms of the once smart Confederate soldiers. She stared at them both and wanted to be sick. Her father looked at her.

'Come on, lass, bestir yourself. Grab his ankles and when I say heave, throw him up on the wagon on top of those sacks of flour.'

'The blood will spoil the flour!'

'No it won't. It's all crusted and dried. Come on now, one, two three . . .'

She used every bit of her puny strength to heave him aboard.

It was only when they got him home and on to a makeshift bed that she saw he was quite handsome behind the dark growth of beard and the yellowish-greenish pallor of his skin. He looked as if the shoulder wound had drained him of blood.

She reckoned he must be nearly thirty, but then soldiers looked older than they really were. It was because of all the terrible experiences they went through, or so Miss Bentley said. It made old men of them. She looked at her father.

'I'll get some hot water to bathe his wound. What will happen to the other man, Pa?'

'We'll sort this one out first, and then I'll go back and bury him. Now let's get on with the job!'

1

Five years had passed since Luke da Souza had left the Lacey ranch. His shoulder had healed slowly. For the first four days he'd lain as one dead and then, one afternoon as Marie-Anne sat with him reading one of Miss Bentley's books, he'd groaned and opened his eyes, looking at her in puzzlement.

'Where am I, and who are you?'

She'd never forgotten the first sight of those tawny-brown eyes as they raked her face.

'I'm Marie-Anne Lacey. Pa and I found you lying off the road when we came home from Sweetwater Butte.'

'Ah, yes . . . ' He'd licked his lips. 'We were ambushed.' Then he struggled to sit up. 'What happened to Ed, my brother Edward?'

She'd looked down at her hands. He

11

looked distraught. It was hard to say.

'He . . . he was dead when we found you.'

'Oh, God!' He'd slumped back on his pillow and closed his eyes. A shiny tear trickled down his cheek and he wiped it away on the back of his hand.

Then he'd looked at her again and saw her youth and innocence and he'd swallowed the burning anger within him.

'I'm hungry and could I have a drink?' For a moment, he was amused at her sudden look of guilt as she shot out of her seat and brought an earthenware mug of milk.

'I'm sorry. I should have offered it to you right away. I'll get you some soup. I've had some special oxtail soup simmering away these last three days.' With a flurry of skirt and petticoat she was gone.

Luke drank the milk gratefully even though he did not enjoy it.

A week later, he forked his horse and

followed John Lacey's directions and visited his brother's grave. He came back quiet and subdued. The next day he shaved off his beard and exchanged his ragged uniform for some of John Lacey's clothes. He shook John's hand and kissed Marie-Anne on the cheek and she wanted to cry because she knew he was leaving.

'I'll never forget you both. You saved my life and anything I can do for you in the future, I will.'

'If you come this way again, drop in at any time. It's been a pleasure having you.' They looked at each other tight-lipped.

'I will. And if you ever need me, you can send a message to Socorro. Anyone there will deliver it.'

'Thank you, Luke. We're all good neighbours in the Sweetwater Valley, but who knows what might come along?'

The five years had not all been good years. For three years now there had been drought at a time when the spring

13

grass should have sprouted. The glut of cows allowed to breed and run wild during the war had now been culled and many had been sent back East to the slaughterhouses, but still there was concern about lack of feed for the cows remaining in the valley.

Amos Jackson's ranch had fared the best, for his cattle roamed the full stretch of Sweetwater Valley on the left side of the Snake River. The Lacey ranch had suffered most because it was situated at the very end of the valley, sharing the land with Thomas Oates and his family. Morton Schofield, who ranched the upper reaches of the valley was rarely short of water, for the Snake River cascaded through the range of mountains to the north and ran crystal clear and pure to tumble down the Sweetwater Valley turning the land to a verdant green.

But that was in the good years. Now, the tumbling whitewater river was dwindling each year into a shallow stream that barely trickled its way to the end of the valley.

The dirt farmers who clustered round the small town of Sweetwater Butte were worried. The three ranchers on the right side of the river were also worried. If the river didn't rise during the next rainy season, then the whole valley could turn into desert and the townsfolk would have to move out.

There had been a meeting in the schoolhouse, chaired by the preacher. Miss Bentley had taken notes, for posterity, she'd explained. She liked things cut and dried and the townsfolk respected her for it.

John Lacey had been there, and Marie-Anne too. It had been exciting for Marie-Anne. She'd never seen so many men and youths gathered together before and even Ellen Beechcroft had been impressed by the choice of young men to flirt with.

Tempers and emotions were high and soon voices were raised after Morton Schofield stood up and told them what he and his riders had found out about the river.

There was a deathly silence as they listened carefully to his findings.

He was a burly man in his forties with receding hair and an aggressive walrus moustache. Now he thrust out his chin and he punched the hat in his hand.

'I'm telling you, men, that the river has been diverted and that part of it has been dammed. It's been done so that it looks like a beaver dam!'

There were catcalls and incredulous shouts of derision.

'If you saw a beaver dam, it must've been a beaver dam! Nobody's goin' to all that trouble to dam the river!'

'Your imagination's runnin' away with you, Morton! Or is it all the booze you drink?' howled another.

'I'm telling you the dam was man-made!'

'And why do you reckon that is?'

The preacher held up his hand for silence while Morton answered.

'Because me and my boys were going to demolish it and we got shot at for our pains. That's why!'

There was an audible gasp running round the room. Then the preacher said quietly, 'Who in God's name would do that?'

Morton Schofield looked slowly at his neighbours' faces.

'Who's not here today or any representative of his family?'

The men looked at each other and then around the room, mentally ticking off everyone they knew. The blacksmith, the storeman, the barber, old Doctor Freeman, the bow-legged ostler and the feed merchant were all there as was Sam from the saloon.

The water question affected everybody and the small dirt farmers in particular for they provided the fruits and vegetables and corn that was needed for the small community.

The preacher stood up straight and tall, his black coat making him seem taller, emphasizing his thick mane of white hair curling about his ears. He looked them all over, deliberately and sure.

'I don't see Mr Jackson or his sons. Are you suggesting that Mr Jackson is responsible for this dwindling of the Snake River?'

'I am, Reverend.'

'This is a serious charge.'

'Which I make in good faith. Any one of you can confirm what me and my boys saw. He can take a ride up the valley and into the foothills of the mountains until he comes to the place where the river now divides. It is but a day's ride. A good man could ride there and be back before daylight.'

The men looked at each other and then they got their heads together and the debate went on.

But there were still those who didn't believe and reckoned Morton Schofield was wrong and that whoever had shot at them must have been owlhooters for it was known that the foothills were crawling with outlaws on the run.

The townsfolk had come to no decision about breaking up the dam when they all dispersed to the saloon to drink and talk it over privately.

John Lacey and Marie-Anne set off for home, John angry that nothing was being done. He was getting desperate. If things didn't improve, they would have to sell their cows and move on. Even the vegetable plot was suffering for their own well was drying up because it was not now being fed by an underground stream from the river.

He looked at Marie-Anne sadly as they unharnessed the horses.

'It looks as if we're going to have to cull the calves. The suckling cows are losing their milk and we can't let the poor beasts starve to death.'

'Oh, no, Pa! I've looked after those calves since the day they were born. They're some of the best we've had!'

'I know, lass. The breeding's good and if the last three years had been good, we'd be well on the way to having a good herd. It's just too much,

19

love. We can't fight nature.'

'But Mr Schofield says it's not nature! Mr Jackson must have started that dam three years ago and it's just grown! There can't have been drought all over those mountains. Even though we haven't had much rain there should have been the meltwater in spring.'

John Lacey looked at her with respect.

'You're a bright lass, Marie-Anne. Morton Schofield's just found out about the dam. Maybe it hasn't occurred to him just how long it's been there. I'll have a word with him next time I'm in town.'

But it was a long time before he got to town.

One morning, while John and the old half-breed Mexican were out mending fences, Amos Jackson and his sons rode into the yard looking for John.

'Where's your father, Marie-Anne?'

Marie-Anne stood on the veranda, her heart beating fast, for she saw Mark

Jackson looking at her as if she was a prize heifer.

'Come on, girl, speak up. Where is he?'

'What do you want him for?'

'That's for him and me to talk over.'

She licked her lips. 'You coming to make trouble? I hear you dammed the river beyond the valley.'

'Oh yeah? That Schofield been spouting his fool head off, has he? Well, let me tell you, miss, he won't do it again. Now where's your father?'

'He's mending the fence near the vegetable patch.'

Amos jerked his head at Hank.

'Go, bring him in. I'm not wasting my time looking for him.'

'No need Amos. What's the reason for this visit?' John Lacey trotted leisurely from behind the barn, followed by the Mexican bringing up the rear with a packhorse carrying all their fencing gear.

He threw a glance at Carlos.

21

'Unpack that gear and rub the horses down before you put 'em in the paddock. I've a feeling we've done all the fencing for today.'

'*Si, señor.*' The old man ambled away, his eyes searching the faces of the three men. He didn't like what he saw.

John Lacey leaned on the pommel of his saddle.

'Well, now, Amos, what's this all about and why is my daughter looking kinda scared?'

'I come as a friend, John. We been neighbours a long time. How many years, John?'

'Nigh on twenty, give or take. Get on with it, man. You sound as if you're winding yourself up. Just spit it out.'

'If that's what you want, John. The plain fact is I want your ranch. I'm offering you five thousand dollars to hightail it from here and that takes in the stock. It's a good offer, John, and Thomas Oates thinks it's a good deal. He leaves within the next few days.'

John stared at him.

'You must be joking, Amos. What gives you the right to walk in here and expect I'll just up sticks and move on just because of your say-so?'

'Five thousand dollars. That's what! Be sensible, John. The drought's got you by the balls and you know it. Another year like this and all your cows will die. You want to see them starve? Look, I'll even make you a better offer. You can come and work for me, and Mark, here — ' and now he grinned, 'has taken a liking for your Marie-Anne. They could set up home here on your ranch. What'd you say to that?'

'I say you can go to hell, Amos Jackson. I never want to see you or your . . . whelps here on my land again! Now get off, or I'll put a bullet in you, so help me God!' He yanked his rifle out of its boot on the horse's flank and cocked it. 'Now be off with you. I mean every word I say!'

Amos Jackson controlled his nervous

animal, a scowl on his face.

'I offered you a fair and square deal, Lacey, and you've thrown it in my face. Now you'll be sorry! You'll come to me begging for me to take your land! And when you do, I'll tell you what to do with it!' He jerked his head at his silent sons, then turned, with a vicious pull on the reins, and rode at a gallop out of the yard, his sons following behind like trailing puppies.

John Lacey watched them until they were out of sight and then uncocked the gun and dismounted stiffly. He gave the reins to Carlos who'd been skulking round the side of the sprawling ranch house. He came to stand beside John.

'There goes one bad man, *señor*. He will be back.' Carlos spat in the dust.

'Yeah, and we'll be ready for him.' Lacey's response was grim.

Marie-Anne clung to one of the veranda's uprights.

'What's it all mean, Pa? What's going on?'

'I think it means war, lass. I've just

bucked Amos Jackson. I never thought a neighbour of such long standing could turn on us small ranchers. It just goes to show you can never trust a man after he gains so much power. It corrupts. But, by God, he'll never ride roughshod over me!'

The days passed and gradually there appeared on the Lacey ranch a growing band of men who sought out Carlos and bedded down with him in the old bunkhouse. A little later, a fat old Mexican woman appeared who introduced herself to John Lacey as the mother of the four strapping sons leading the little band, and that she was going to cook for them.

'What the hell are all these relatives of yours doing here, Carlos? I can't afford to pay them wages.'

'They're not here for wages, *señor*. They're here to protect me and, of course, you and the *señorita*, too. Your wages to me have helped to support them for years. Now they help me. We all are satisfied!'

John Lacey shook his head doubtfully. 'Well, if you and they are satisfied, I can sure use their help, but I only hope nobody gets hurt!'

'They are protected, *señor*. Juanita goes to the village every Sunday and puts candles on the altar of the church and prays for us all. We've got the power of the Almighty all around us. Bullets won't hit us, *señor*. I know it!' Carlos grinned at John Lacey. He was so confident, it hurt. John Lacey sighed.

'Your belief in God is good and great, but I don't believe God Himself can protect us if Amos Jackson keeps that water dammed upriver.'

'Then we go and undam river. Very simple.'

'But it is more than a hundred miles' ride, Carlos. Jackson isn't going to be sitting on his ass twiddling his thumbs.'

Carlos shrugged thin shoulders.

'I'm too old to ride, but there are those amongst us who will go and do this thing. I will see to it.'

'If you are determined on this plan . . . '

'My sister's sons have already talked about it. The river affects their village too, you know. The Snake River is the lifeblood of the very valley itself. Already there are many changes for the small tributaries have now dried up and the springs around three villages have already turned to mudholes. Something must be done.'

'All right, Carlos, I leave it in your hands, but tell those nephews of yours to be careful.'

'I will. The boys have a great incentive to succeed and return as heroes. Certain girls from the villages have promised marriage despite the boys having no pigs or burros to give to their fathers!'

Suddenly, overnight, half the men in the bunkhouse were gone. John Lacey deemed it best not to ask questions but thought it necessary to go to town and ask for the latest news concerning the ranchers and the dirt farmers.

'Pa, I want to go with you!'

'Not this time, lass. Carlos and his troops will look after you. God knows what it will be like in Sweetwater Butte, but I'll bring back extra dry goods and we'll fort up just in case Carlos's boys aren't as clever as they think they are.'

'You think Amos Jackson will have guards watching the dam?'

'Yeah, wouldn't you in the circumstances? The goddamn feller's no fool and he's got the men to do it.'

'Pa, I'm frightened.'

'No need to be. We've got all this side of the valley backing us. Jackson can't just steamroller over us all.'

'But you said there were folks moving out because of the drought.'

'Yeah, Oates and his family have gone, and a few of the poorer dirt farmers.'

'Pa, have you thought about Oates's place? It's slap bang in between us and Mr Schofield's spread. Maybe Jackson's got men on it already?'

John Lacey scratched his chin.

'Never thought of that.'

'It would mean we're cut off from the rest of the valley. We've got to pass their road in when we go to town. There could be guards there . . . ' Her voice trailed away.

For a moment there was a long silence and then John Lacey said heavily, 'There's only one thing to do. Go and find out!'

Marie-Anne swung round to face him.

'Pa, isn't it time we sent a message to Socorro?'

They stared at each other.

'You think we should send for Luke da Souza?'

She nodded. 'You remember what he said. Any time we needed help, he would come.'

'That was five years ago. Maybe he's forgotten us now.'

'He wasn't that kind of man. I *know* he will come!'

'Right. I'll get Carlos to send a messenger. We can but try!'

2

The two guards sat with backs against a huge rock, sharing a bottle of whiskey, drinking alternately from the bottle. They were easy and careless. It had been days since Amos Jackson had ordered them and the Madison brothers to watch, turn and turn about.

It was lonely and monotonous and the two men missed the chores of the ranch and the bickering of the men and the occasional fight that relieved the boredom of ranch life. They also got on each other's nerves. Willy had a way of whistling through his teeth that angered Chuck Masters, and he disgusted Willy by breaking wind when he was near him and the stink was foul.

'I don't know why the hell we're here,' grumbled Chuck. 'Those fools down in the valley haven't got the brains to figure out the real trouble.

Nobody will come all the way up here to investigate.'

'Morton Schofield found out and he's no fool.'

'But nobody believed him and, sure as hell, there's been no rush for the fools to come and see for themselves. We might as well go back to the ranch.'

'And take a rollicking from the boss? Hell! We might just as well pack up and get outa this cursed valley! Jackson's a bastard when he's crossed. Strikes me he's gone loco since that boy of his was killed. Anyone opposes him, he erupts like a blasted volcano.'

'Hmm, I never knew Abe Jackson. He was before my time. It's said he was a wild 'un and the old man's pride and joy.'

'Yeah. The stallion amongst the geldings as it were. These Jacksons ain't a patch on Abe. I knew him when we was both knee-high to a grasshopper. He got the idea of going off to war and being a hero and nothing would

31

stop him. Though old Amos yelled and threatened, the boy must go and he took his brothers with him.' He put his head close to Chuck's. 'Between you and me, those boys aren't worth shit! It was said they all went running when they fought at Petersburg and they saw Lee was being beaten by Grant, after some of their comrades broke ranks. A damned officer shot Abe dead. Ned was lucky. He lost his arm, but it saved his life. The other two . . . ' He shrugged contemptuously. 'Shit their pants I expect and laid doggo until the danger was over.'

'Rumour has it in the bunkhouse that the boys waylaid the officer and shot him and his brother.'

'Yeah, I've heard the rumour. I bet it was old Amos who did it, or if it wasn't, then he scared hell out of the boys to make 'em do it! I never knew such a litter of helpless whelps!'

They both laughed and took another swig each from the bottle which was now nearly empty.

'Nearly chow time. The boys will be here soon.'

'And not before time. I could do with some of Cookie's stew.'

Chuck held up the bottle to see how much was left. Dusk was coming down quickly in the cleft of the hills where the Snake River had gradually worn a passage. The lingering light on the bottle made it gleam fitfully, and then, all of a sudden, it exploded and Chuck was left holding a jagged bottle neck. The report of a gun echoed amongst the jagged cliffs.

'What the hell?' Both men sprang to their feet and looked about them in panic.

Nothing stirred, but over the river rose a lazy plume of smoke.

'Holy hell!' gasped Chuck, 'That was nearly my goddamned hand!' He peered into the gloom of trees that clung precariously in the cracks of ancient boulders, but nothing moved. He moved into the shadows where Willy was crouching.

'What do we do now, Willy?'

'Let whoever's out there think we've been hurt when he tries again. This is going to be a waiting game, Chuck. Someone's going to come out down there where the dam starts and try breaking it up. That's when we start shooting. When he shoots back we'll give a yell and he will think he's got a hit.'

'Then we should split up and when he shows himself, we can nail him.'

'You got the idea, son. He must be a lone hunter or else we would have heard 'em coming.'

But Willy was wrong and he didn't live long enough to know it.

Chuck stepped out into the open to take a good look at the dam and a bullet spat viciously, catching him in the shoulder. His yell was real and Willy lunged for him to save him from falling down the deep gorge. He clutched Chuck and then the world exploded in his face and the small group of men below watched the two men plummet into the Snake River.

Carlos's four nephews cheered as did the half-dozen men accompanying them. It had been as easy as shooting tin cans off a log. The old devil had been right. There'd been guards and now there were none and they could get to the task of breaking open the dam and letting the water flow freely.

They cheered and there was a mad scramble to get to the riverbank.

They used dead branches and their bare hands to heave the mass of rotting debris interwoven into a thick mattress of leaves and grasses and twigs weighted down with sugarbags filled with sand and grit that had been deliberately placed at the narrowest part of the river. They started in the middle, and the men plunged in despite the coldness of the water to allow the first scummy water to flow freely.

There were yells of triumph as the flow became stronger, taking loosened debris with it.

Far above them, a bunch of horsemen watched grimly.

'What we going to do, Pa?' Mark Jackson watched the expressions move across his father's face. He dreaded the outbursts of maniacal rage.

They had heard the gunfire from a distance. The Madison brothers had just left them to relieve the other guards. They and Amos and his line gang, already tired after a day's work shoring up fences and mending gaps, galloped towards the dam.

Now they watched as the work of destruction went on.

'Can you see anything of Chuck and Willy?' Amos asked his foreman who was looking through his glasses to try and identify the men down below.

'No sign of them, boss, but those fellers down below are some of Lacey's half-breed, Carlos's kin. There's Mexes and Indians down there and if we tangle with them, there could be a wholesale uprising. What d'you think, boss?'

Les Shincliffe was a wary man. He didn't approve of all of Amos's ideas and the man's callous indifference to life. If the old man's idea of taking over the whole of the Sweetwater Valley meant that men were going to be killed for it, then he was going to collect his dues and ride out. He wasn't going to risk his life for a crazy old coot like Jackson.

'To hell with 'em! I don't care a hell-spitting preacher's cuss for any stinking half-breeds. We'll give 'em a salvo now to surprise the bastards, then go down there and shove the rest in the river. That'll warn the townsfolk not to interfere as the bodies start drifting down!'

'But, boss . . . .'

'If you don't like the way things are going, Les, just pack your gear and git! But don't come crawling back for your job when the all clear comes!' He turned in his saddle and shouted and waved.

'All right, boys! A bonus for everyone

you hit! Think of them as rats down there, and don't spare the bullets!'

A great howl went up and the guns and rifles spat and the bullets buzzed like angry hornets. Down below, a man heaving up a dripping sack full of rocks suddenly stiffened and the shirt on his back turned red. He gasped and gurgled as he slumped into the water. He was the first man to be hit.

Then, one by one, the others fell, engulfed by the red-stained water, until only those on the bank remained.

But now they had overcome their first surprise and had taken shelter and were firing back. It was a vicious battle and, as Les Shincliffe watched from the shelter of a rock, he saw three of Jackson's men fall into the river below.

That was it, Les told himself. He would never again work for Amos Jackson. Sure, he'd done some things that he was ashamed of in his time, but he never classed himself as a murderer. He quietly made tracks, leading his horse until he was well away from the scene. He had no stomach for an all-out gun war and he could see that that was what it was going to be.

He'd get as far away from Sweetwater Valley as he could go and to hell with them all.

Down below, Carlos's nephew, Ferengo, cursed as he watched his brother Georgio drift away on the current. There was no time to plunge into the water and try and drag him to the bank. He was being outmanoeuvred by two of Jackson's gunnies. He couldn't move from behind his rock because the bastards were using him for target practice. All around him were the new chipped marks of bullets. At this rate, he thought sourly, they're going to run out of ammunition. It was going to cost them plenty to kill him!

Then, suddenly, they were gone and a deathly silence enveloped the gorge. The dam was still in place but it had been breached and a gap about eight feet wide was funnelling the water through like a millrace.

Ferengo stuck his hat on the end of his rifle and waved it above his rock. Nothing happened. He threw a stone and there was no sharp retort. He stood up and looked around. The only movement came from those left alive down near the river's edge.

They crawled out from their temporary bunkers, shaken and bloody, looking about them fearfully. It could be all a trick.

Ferengo came down, taking long strides and joining his brother Jonas.

'They got Georgio.'

Jonas nodded. 'And Blue Billy.'

Ferengo showed his teeth in anger. 'We'll get 'em. We'll go back and tell the others and we'll fire the bastard's ranch!'

Jonas looked worried. 'Is that wise? Amos Jackson has an army of men, and he's got a reputation for revenge. He could fire the villages and the women and children would suffer.'

'We'll talk about it with *Señor* Lacey.

He'll know what to do.'

It was a bedraggled, vengeful bunch who returned to the Lacey ranch. John Lacey, watching them ride in, saw at a glance that several of the village men were missing, including Georgio and Blue Billy. His anger against Amos Jackson mounted.

The villagers waited outside while Ferengo and Jonas went indoors to report what had happened to John Lacey.

'So what Morton Schofield said was true! Those bastards deliberately dammed the river just below the fork so that most of the water was diverted to Jackson's side of the valley. Goddamn him for a murderer! We can lay the deaths of those men at his door!'

Marie-Anne came into the living-room from the kitchen and the two brothers nodded shyly in acknowledgement of her.

'Pa, Carlos is in the kitchen. I think you should talk to him. He says he's heard of the deaths and is very upset.'

'Send him in, Marie-Anne. God knows how he's going to break the news to the families concerned! It should be my responsibility. They did it for me and the other ranchers and townsfolk in the valley.'

Carlos shuffled into the room and for the first time, John Lacey realized that Carlos was showing his age.

'I'm sorry, Carlos. I don't know what to say.' He clapped the old man on the back. There were tears in the old man's eyes.

'They were all good men and you don't need to feel guilt for they were defending the rights of their villages just as you are defending the life of this ranch. Water is the right of every living man and whoever tries to control the water supply is going against God and man. Amos Jackson will rue the day he flouted the laws of nature!

'Tomorrow I'll ride into town and organize another meeting and this time it will not be just talk, but a planning of action. Morton Schofield was right

42

and we should have trusted him. We wasted time, but now we shall have to hit back.'

But it was too late for some. Already Jackson's hit squad was out terrorizing the dirt farmers who were helpless against the mob violence. Hayricks were fired and one ranch house was burned to the ground. Fences were broken down and livestock scattered.

When John Lacey rode into town, the mood was ugly and there was talk of recruiting an army and crossing the river and burning the ranch house, lynching Amos Jackson and his sons and shooting down any of the crew who resisted.

'Sweep the valley clean of the Devil's spawn!' raved old Tag Tindel, his eyes flashing and his long grey beard springing up all around him as he waved his arms and punched the air. He it was who'd had to stand helplessly and watch as his hayrick and his smithy burned to the ground.

John Lacey stood on a box and raised

his hands into the air in an effort to calm them so that he might speak.

'Hold your horses everyone. We've got to do this legal. I've got a man coming any day now, to help us.'

'Is he a lawman?' someone shouted.

'No. But he was a major in the army.'

'That doesn't mean much! Any fool with the cash to pay could buy his way into the army!' There was much laughter at this as they all remembered the private platoons rigged and paid for by the rich slave owners, who hadn't the least idea how to command their men or take orders from those who did.

'Luke da Souza was military trained. He fought well for the Confederates and was an aide to General Lee. He'll know how to root out Amos Jackson and his crew of gunnies.'

A ragged cheer rang out, but there were many who shook their heads.

'But will he come too late?' boomed Tag Tindel. 'I've already lost all I've

44

worked for for the last thirty years!'

There was no answer to that. They would have to wait and see.

* * *

Carlos stood behind Marie-Anne as the stranger trotted into the yard. He rode with casual grace, straight-backed, rifle laid across the pommel as if he was always on guard.

He wore a wide Mexican sombrero pulled well down over his eyes. His face was darkly shadowed, but she was aware of a thin moustache that curved about his mouth. He wore a scuffed leather jerkin over a thick black shirt and his pants were also of leather. His high boots were black and well polished and silver spurs tinkled as he moved.

Two bandoleers criss-crossed his chest and a low-slung gunbelt showed the polished ivory handles of two well-used guns.

He smiled.

Marie-Anne was rooted to the spot.

Her heart fluttered. This was the man she'd nursed five years ago. She'd known her father had sent for him, but she never really believed he would come.

'You're Marie-Anne. You remember me? The man from Socorro?'

She nodded, her tongue cleaving to the roof of her mouth. She felt a fool.

'I've come because your father sent for me.'

Carlos glanced at her and then stepped forward.

'The messenger was one of my nephews, *señor*. There is much trouble in the valley.'

'I see that you have been badly hit by the drought and that your irrigation channels are dried up. That is very bad luck, *señor*. If that is the trouble, how does Mr Lacey expect me to help?'

'That is not the trouble, *señor*. It is how the remaining water has been diverted. On the other side of the river there is but one big ranch and the owner is taking advantage of the drought by making things worse by concentrating the water to irrigate his land.'

'I see. If I remember when I was here last, the river spread across the flat marshy areas and became streams and then came together as one when it left the valley and so there was plenty of grass to feed the herds.'

Carlos nodded. 'That is so, *señor*. But now all has changed. We blamed the drought, but one of the ranchers on this side of the river made his way upstream beyond the valley and into the mountains and found out that the river had been dammed, thus starving us of water.'

'But it would be simple to tear down the dam?'

'Yes, *señor*, but the dam is guarded and already some of our men have been killed. Amos Jackson and his sons are ruthless men.'

'Amos Jackson, you say?'

'Yes. Since the war he has built a

huge ranch house high on a plateau that juts out halfway up yonder hills. His land unfolds before him and he can view his herds from his veranda. It is a regular fort and it is guarded by his men at all times.'

Luke da Souza's eyes gleamed.

'I once knew four men by the name of Jackson. One died during the battle of Petersburg before the surrender.'

Carlos looked sly. 'Would he have been Abe Jackson?'

Luke da Souza pursed his lips. 'I believe that was his name.'

Carlos looked at him with new respect.

'Then you killed one of the Jackson litter!'

Luke da Souza frowned. 'Then it must have been the Jacksons who waylaid us and shot me and killed my brother!' He sighed and then roused himself. 'But this is no time for talking about the past. I must talk to Mr Lacey.'

Marie-Anne had stood quietly pulling

herself together. Now she said softly, 'You'll be hungry. If you would come inside I'll see that you get something to eat and drink.'

'Thank you, ma'am.' He dismounted and Carlos led the horse away. Marie-Anne's cheeks dimpled as she smiled at the ma'am. It wasn't often she was addressed as ma'am. It made her feel really grown up.

'Just call me Marie-Anne,' she said shyly.

His eyes twinkled. 'You're all grown up. I wasn't sure what to call you. Marie-Anne seemed disrespectful.'

He followed her up on to the veranda and bent his head to pass through the door. Inside, he looked about him. Nothing had changed. It was just as he remembered it.

She indicated a chair by the fire. He sat down and stretched out his feet towards the open log fire.

'This is nice. To settle into a comfortable chair before a roaring fire after a hard day's riding.' As she poured a mug of homemade ale and offered it, he said quietly so that she just heard the words, 'It's heaven.'

Then she was bustling about bringing out fresh bread, warming leftover stew on a hook over the fire and seeking a whole new succulent cheese just ready for eating.

Then she was watching him eat, as the old coffeepot brewed up and the fragrance of coffee filled the room. She shared a cup of coffee with him when he'd sat back replete.

He was telling her of his life in Socorro and his easy way of talking relaxed her and she forgot to be shy. They were laughing about his humorous tale of branding calves and being butted in the backside by an irate mother, when John Lacey walked in.

'Luke!'

'John, it's good to see you again!' Both men embraced.

'It's been a long time!'

'Too long. The years fly by. What's this trouble I hear about?'

John told him how trouble had flared between Amos Jackson and the rest of the valley settlers while Marie-Anne bustled about making fresh coffee for all of them and rustling up a quick meal for her father.

She watched and listened, most of her attention on the tall, dark man she remembered. Now he looked a little older. There was some grey in the hair at his temples but he was tanned and fit and moved easily. The thin gaunt man of her dreams was gone. This was the man she remembered and yet he was not. But he still made her heart flutter.

She wondered if he was married but dared not ask.

Then she was conscious of some argument going on between the two. She listened.

'The idea's absurd! You can't go alone up there on Jackson land and face them on your own!'

'Why not? It's my fight as well as yours. I've told you that I'm

51

convinced we were bushwhacked by the Jacksons. We were passing through their country when it happened. They must have been following us and took their chances, so that they could get clean away to their ranch and all have alibis if they were needed.'

'But, Luke . . . '

'They got away with it, didn't they? You found us. You brought me here and you buried Ed. There was no hue and cry because all hell was popping at that time with the surrender and all. Now, it is different. I'm going after them, John, and nothing you can say will stop me!'

'And get yourself killed,' John said bitterly. 'You have no idea how many men are up there. Amos must have been planning this takeover years ago. Everyone in the valley is ready to fight. All we want is a leader with some know-how. You could be that man, Luke.'

'And be responsible for a lot of deaths! Do you want that? It could turn out real bloody, John. No, far better for me to go in and cut off the snake's head. That way the rest of the body dies!'

Marie-Anne listened and her heart froze. She didn't want this man exposed to the danger of going off on his own.

'Luke, please! Listen to Pa. At least take some men with you who know the land.'

'Yes, the lass is right, Luke. Even a couple of men who know the country would give you a better chance.'

Luke was thoughtful.

'Maybe two me . . . ' he began, as Marie-Anne interrupted.

'You should take Ferengo and Jonas along with you. They know the country like Indians and their brothers were killed, too. They have a right to go after the Jacksons. Isn't that so, Pa?'

'Yeah, I suppose so, but I would much rather have sent all the available men in the valley.'

'And started an all-out war. It could

go on forever, John, and I'm sick of war. By God, if you'd been in the last, you would never even think of involving everyone.'

'But it's their fight too!'

'Let's try it my way, first. You sent for me; now let me do the thinking.'

'And you'll take Ferengo and Jonas?'

'If they volunteer to come.'

'They'll volunteer all right. Killing Georgio and Blue Billy makes it their business.'

'Right. I'll talk to them in the morning. Meanwhile, with your permission I'd like to go and visit my brother's grave.'

'Certainly. Do you want me to show you the way?'

'Nope! If you point me in the direction, I'll find it.'

John respected his need for privacy. He went outside with him and watched while Luke saddled up and then said, 'If you ride due west until you come to a small hill with a dead tree on the top of it, you'll find Ed's grave at its foot. Oh, and Luke . . . '

'Yes, John?'

'I just wanted to say, thanks for coming and I'd sure like hell not want to see you hurt. You won't take any fool chances when you go over the river?'

Luke gazed down at him and laughed as he made himself comfortable in the saddle.

'I enjoy life too much to want to cut it short. Be assured, John, I'm no gambler when it comes to surviving! I'll not do anything heroic, believe me!'

John nodded. He was satisfied.

It didn't take long for Luke to spy the stark dead tree that spread dead branches, like fingers, into the air. It stood out even in the gathering dusk.

Luke dismounted and walked the short distance until he found the grave. Then, hobbling the horse, he went and knelt down beside the carefully tended mound and put his hand where Ed's chest might be.

'I'm back, Ed. I'm sorry I didn't

come sooner, but I haven't stopped thinking about you and the good times we had together. It's payback time now, Ed, and I'm gonna see that they're paid back with interest! They know and you and I know that there was more to it than just those bastards deserting. It's time old Amos Jackson knew just what kind of cubs he raised!'

He sat back on his haunches and lit a cheroot and contemplated the surrounding country and watched a thin new moon sail across the sky. It could be a good country, green and fertile if the rains came in time and the river was allowed free flood again.

He could see why the ranchers and farmers of Sweetwater Valley were willing to fight for their land. No man had the right to take what was not his and turn other people off their own properties.

He had a vision of Amos Jackson dressed in red and with horns surrounded by fire and his sons leaping around him as the flames rose and fell and grew stronger because there was no one to stop the Devil's power.

He turned once again to face the grave.

'I'll stop the bastards, or I'll come and join you, Ed, I swear!' He got up and felt curiously strong as if Ed answered him on the cool breeze.

'I know you can do it, Luke. You could always do anything you put your mind to when we were kids. Good luck, Luke!'

He rode away, his mind busy on how to tackle the breaching of the ranch in military fashion. What would General Lee have recommended, if he'd been in charge?

He knew, of course. Send in the special agents, armed to the teeth with every known weapon and the skill of the country. Well, if the half-breeds were as skilful as John Lacey said, then they were halfway there. The rest was up to him.

3

Amos Jackson rapped the long refectory table with hard knuckles. He was angry and when Amos was angry, everyone sat up and listened.

The row of faces looked at him with certain degrees of fear, respect and alarm. The boss had been as bitter as gall since that lily-livered Les Shincliffe had sloped off, not even going back to collect his gear or claim his pay. Not that the rest of the crew minded, they'd divided out his stuff and shrugged him out of their lives.

But now old Amos was having to make do with Mark as the new foreman and Mark sure wasn't up to scratch. Now he was looking red and uncomfortable and, below the surface, an ugly anger was festering.

'I'm only telling you what I heard in town, Pa. One of Lacey's half-breed hangers-on was shooting off his mouth. He says Luke da Souza is back in the valley. That's all I know.'

'Why didn't you get him on one side and find out where he was holing up? Jesus! Have you no brains in that head of yours?' Mark stared sullenly at his dirty plate. 'And the rest of you, don't you ever listen to what's bandied about in the saloon?'

An over-fat, bald-headed man spoke up defiantly.

'You forget, boss, we're not welcome in town and you know why. Any of us poke our noses in there and we'd be lynched! We haven't got a decent drinking den any more and I for one am getting fed up with the situation.'

'Yeah, and me too,' spoke up another, inspired by the other man's outburst.

'What you want me to do? Supply you with free liquor as well as the bonuses I promised you?'

The man who'd protested about losing his drinking place, brightened.

'Would you do that, boss? We could build us a new bunkhouse in no time and maybe you could bring in a few women and then it would be home from home!'

Amos Jackson roared and thumped the table.

'What in hell is this? I'm out to build myself an empire and willing to pay all the crew well, but I'm damned if I'm pussy-footing around with a lot of fairies who grouse about the lack of drinking facilities! It was bad enough Les walking out. If any of you feel the way he did, then say so now and you can be on your way!' He stared at each one in turn. 'Well?'

They looked at him and then at each other and then down at their plates.

'You're a lot of stinking yellow-bellies! And as for you three . . .' He looked over his three sons with contempt. 'I don't know who the hell you lot take after! Not one of you is like me. Only Abe; and that goddamned da Souza shot him dead! He's back here because you and Hank didn't finish the job.' He glared at Mark. 'You rode away without checking . . . '

Mark stood up in a fury.

'We got Ed da Souza, didn't we? And we shot the major out of the saddle. He rolled and didn't move and there was a wagon coming along the road in the distance. We had to get away fast. That's what you would have done, isn't it? I'm sick of you getting at us for everything! Hank and me have been your slaves long enough!'

Amos Jackson leaned over the table thrusting out his chin, eyes glaring.

'And what are you going to do about it? Walk out like Les Shincliffe with nothing? Believe me, if you do go, I'll see you leave my land stripped naked! And you've got my word on it!'

Mark gulped and turned white and sat down as all eyes turned to him. This was something to talk about in the bunkhouse during the customary games of poker.

Hank stood up. He looked at a silent

Ned who sat quietly, his empty sleeve pinned down. He usually kept well away from his father for the sight of the empty sleeve held a revulsion for the old man.

'Pa,' said Hank, 'there's something you should know.'

'What's that, boy? What don't I know?'

'Abe wasn't all you thought he was. He was . . . ' He stopped and looked at Ned who looked away. Ned was no help.

'What about Abe? He had something none of you lot have. The boy had guts!'

Hank bit his lip. 'He and Ned were shot as deserters . . . '

'I know all about that lying crap put out by the army. Abe would never be a deserter. Now Ned there, might well have been, but not Abe!'

Ned sprang to his feet, his white thin face taking on a ruddy hue.

'Goddammit, Pa! Why don't you take the blinders off your eyes? We've never told you the true story why Major da Souza shot us! It wasn't just that the four of us deserted during the Battle of Petersburg. Lots of men were running away. They left in droves to save their lives. It was because your precious Abe sold us all out! He even sold *us* out and I lost my arm through him! May he rot in Hell!'

There was a terrible silence. It was as if all the listening men held their breath at once. A fly could be heard buzzing its wings at the window. Nothing stirred.

Then came the roar.

'You lying, snivelling bastard! If you weren't my son I'd kill you for saying that!' There was anguish in his tones. He was like a wounded lion. He looked at the staring men. 'Get out of here! And if any man talks about this I'll string him up and crack his balls!'

The men climbed over the long benches and slunk out of the old kitchen, leaving the sons behind.

Amos Jackson stood, a bowed figure, and appraised them all. Ned, as the

oldest of the three, he hardly looked at.
It hurt too much to see him so much
less of a man. Of Mark and Hank,
perhaps Mark was the brightest but
not by much. Amos sat down heavily.
His voice came as a croak. He spoke
to Ned but didn't look at him.

'You're lying, aren't you? You're
doing this because of your ma and
Abe isn't here to refute your claims.'

Ned laughed bitterly.

'You don't have to believe me. Ask
them. They know. And keep Ma out
of this. She's dead and at peace and
how you treated her is between you
and God.'

The old man looked at Hank and
Mark who stared him in the eye. Amos
went to the window and stared out at
the verdant pastures on his side of the
valley. Then he whirled around and
came to stand before them.

'Abe spied for the Yankees, didn't
he?' Ned looked at him resolutely.

'Yes.'

'They paid him?'

64

'Yes.'

'He helped to lose the Battle of Petersburg and helped to bring about the surrender?'

'Yes, and Major da Souza got wind of it. By then Abe was insistent that we should flee. It seemed a good idea to us all. We didn't know what he knew, however. We scattered, but I remained with him and lost my arm. You always thought the sun shone out of Abe's ass but none of us thought our oldest brother was a little tin god. We knew what he really was. Now *you* know.'

The old man nodded.

'At least he had guts!' His eyes roved contemptuously over them all. 'I wonder which one of you will stand up to the major when he comes looking for you?' He laughed. 'It should be interesting, for he'll surely come hunting. That's why he's here. I'm surprised he's waited five years to do it.'

The brothers looked at each other. Mark said softly, 'We shouldn't wait for him to find us, we should go looking for him.'

'Now you're thinking more like a man,' Amos said approvingly. 'Maybe there's a bit of me in one of you, after all.' He walked to the door and then looked back at them all. 'This valley, when I own it all, will only be left to one of you, so figure it out, boys, which one will it be?'

Ned cursed when he'd gone.

'The swine! He's never been a father to us! He always blamed Ma for being sweet on that Bert Weldon who disappeared. You remember him?'

Mark nodded. Hank looked confused but interested.

'What about him?' he asked, looking from Mark to Ned.

'He was Pa's foreman and friend for years. Then when you were about two and a bit, he disappeared. Just went off in the blue. I remember there was a lot of shouting. Ma standing up to Pa during the night. I woke up and listened. She was screaming at him. It's a wonder you both didn't wake up. Abe did and he went to their room and was told to get to hell out of it.'

'But *why* . . . ?' Hank began.

'Because none of us looked like Pa, dimwit! Only Abe had his dark looks; we take after Ma.'

'But Bert couldn't have been our father!' Mark broke in. 'If he had been, he would never have left us.'

Ned looked at him pityingly.

'Maybe he didn't leave. Maybe he was bush-whacked and shoved into a hole!' There was a long, painful silence.

Then Hank whispered softly, 'You think Pa killed him?'

Ned shrugged. 'I was only a little kid at the time, but Ma swore on the life of all of us that Amos was our father. But he was never sure. That's why he used to beat her up when he came home drunk.'

'And that's why we're all scared of him, isn't it?' Hank said bitterly. 'We know what he's capable of, and

God help me, he made us all what we are!'

'Except Abe, who always went his own way.'

'Because Pa never showed him his rough side.'

Mark looked at them both.

'So what do we do now?'

'Same as always. Go along with what he wants,' Ned said sadly. 'I'm out of it. It's up to you and Hank, Mark. We're all just puppets and he pulls the strings.'

'What about this da Souza? D'you think he's come back especially to find us? He'll be out for revenge.'

'It's all I can figure, you two will have to watch your backs.'

'As I said before, we should go and find him first.' For once Mark resembled his father. 'I'll go talk to the old man.'

Mark found his father in the main bunkhouse talking to the men.

'So that's the way I see it, boys. We start with the townsfolk. Ransack the stores and hostelry, kill the trade and the townsfolk will scatter. Then we start with Schofield and clear his ranch and work through the farmers. If they can't get supplies, they have a choice of leaving or fighting it out.'

'What about John Lacey at the lower end of the valley?' someone asked. Amos Jackson hesitated.

'He's a long-time neighbour and I'd rather he just moved on. I want to talk to him and make him see reason. We'll leave him until last.'

'What about this da Souza you were talking about?' another asked. 'Something about him killing your Abe, wasn't it?'

'Ah, yes, da Souza. If any of you come across a big man who's a stranger to you, I want him taken prisoner so I can look him over. If he's caught, there's a bonus for the man who brings him in.'

'I take it he's a dangerous, trigger-happy, bastard?' the man asked.

Mark stepped forward.

'You can all forget da Souza. Hank and I are going after him ourselves.'

Amos looked at him with surprise and scepticism.

'How long you been skulking out there listening, boy?'

Mark flushed. He detested the way his father reduced him to a little boy in front of the men. Now he was supposed to take Len Shincliffe's place as foreman, and yet his father would not give him the respect that went with the job.

'I've just come over from the house. I suppose it didn't occur to you that as foreman I should have been here at the beginning of this meeting?'

Amos frowned. 'Getting a little cocky, aren't we? Let me tell you I'm still boss of this spread and I can do as I damn well like! And just to remind you and to be a lesson to everyone, I'll give you this, free and gratis!' He swung his fist around and caught the unsuspecting Mark on the chin.

Mark went backwards and slammed

over one of the men's cots and landed in a heap on the bare boards behind.

A couple of the men rushed to haul him upright, but Amos lifted a hand.

'Leave him! Let the little bastard come to where he is. He needs a lesson in what's due to me. You fellers, be ready to ride out at daybreak!' He swept outside and back to the main ranch.

The men looked at each other and one of them spat on the floor.

'Or to hell! Let's get him up. Mark's done us no harm and if someone sneaks and tells the old man, I'll personally whip the hide off him myself! You would think we were all frightened of the old devil!'

Two of the men hauled Mark upright and sat him on a chair. His head lolled and a huge swelling bruise was showing on his chin. They sloshed whiskey down his neck until he choked and shook his head and blinked his eyes.

'Wha-what happened?'

'Your old man put one on your

chin. A regular blinder. How're you feeling, pal?'

'Like I been trodden on by a herd of cows.'

'You'll live,' said the oldest man in the crew. 'Just keep out of the way for a few days. That's my advice, son.'

'Like hell I will!' Mark tried to stand up but his legs were like jelly. He collapsed back on the chair. 'Jesus! I feel as if my head's been busted!'

In the ranch house, Ned and Hank watched their father go to his desk and bring out a bottle of whiskey and pour a huge measure. In silence they watched while he gulped it down and poured another. There was a twitch at the corner of his mouth.

Then Hank found the courage to ask, 'Where's Mark?'

Amos drained the glass and turned swiftly and threw it with some fury into the fireplace. The pieces tinkled as they hit the brickwork and showered down over the hearth.

'Where you both should be: in the

bunkhouse. Where else?'

Hank wet his lips. 'Why is he there, Pa?'

'Because the bastard tried to tell me what he was going to do. I give the orders around here so I put him in his place.'

'I'll go find him.'

'You'll do no such thing! I gave orders for him to stay where he was. It's a lesson for him. One he'll never forget!'

Just then there was a scrabble at the door. It opened and slammed back against the wall; Mark clung on to the jamb, swaying. There was a mad look in his eyes.

'You'll be sorry for this, Pa!' And he collapsed face down. Hank and Ned rushed to pick him up and, when they did so, saw the livid bruise on his chin.

'What happened to him, Pa?'

'He was cocky, but he's got a glass jaw just like both of you! None of you are real men . . . ' That was when Ned hit him and the punch from his one arm was just as strong and vicious as his father's. There were long years of hate and resentment in that one blow and as Amos's breath blasted from him as he collapsed on the floor, Ned took a running kick at his ribs.

Hank restrained him.

'Hold on, Ned, or you'll kill him!'

Ned breathed hard. 'He should have died years ago!'

'But you don't want to be the one to do it! You wouldn't want to live with the knowledge you killed your own father!'

'I wish to God, Bert Weldon had been our pa! Anyone would have been better than him!' Ned ran his fingers through his hair. His hand was shaking. 'Come on, let's do something for Mark. We'll do something for that old devil later.'

4

Luke da Souza, with Ferengo and Jonas, looked down on the remains of the dam. They were as near the gorge as they could get on horseback. The horses pawed fretfully, disturbed by the rushing water below and the wheeling and calling of birds around them.

They watched for Jackson's guards. The sheer cliffs on both sides at the narrowing of the river made it a funnel as the water tumbled and raced through the narrow opening.

'So what we'll do, boys, is round up the guards and make 'em build another dam letting this water through but blocking the tributary that runs through Jackson's land. How far upriver is the fork, Ferengo?'

'Not more than a mile, *señor*. Those cliffs on the other side are a humpback ridge and the water's carved a way around it. It joins up again with the main river outside the Sweetwater Valley way past the Lacey spread. That's why we need this part of the river flowing free. It's the lifeblood of the valley.'

'Hmm, so we'll have to figure a way down there, capture the guards and finish what you fellers started.'

Ferengo grinned.

'We know the way down. It's an old Indian trail and used regularly by some of our villagers. It leads right into the mountains and to the Indian mountain villages.'

'Good. Then you can lead the way.'

It took several hours to lead the horses step by step down the steep trail and tether them some distance away. Then they doubled back and moved cautiously towards the dam.

They were in time to watch the changeover. Two men had ridden in and were now squatting around a small fire, drinking coffee while the two guards relieved of duty packed their gear on their horses.

'Anyone pass this way?' asked one, who was a burly man with a gut.

'Nah! It's all a waste of time. The old man's loco and if he didn't pay good, I'd be off,' answered one of the men strapping down his kit on his horse's rump.

'He still thinks those ranchers will try another sortie.'

'Like hell they will! They haven't got a leader. They're just a lot of bleaters,' said the first man. 'Those ranchers can't last much longer and if the boss goes ahead with his plan, then they'll not even be able to get any stores. They'll be starved out by the drought and lack of food.'

'Well, I say it's a shame,' said the second man drinking coffee and crouching by the fire. 'The old buzzard had plenty of land on this side of the river. Those folks on the other side have worked damned hard for what they've got!'

'Don't let Jackson hear you say that, Smithy. He don't like anyone to have different opinions to his own.'

Smithy shrugged. 'I'm only saying what a lot of you men think. We're not all tarred with Jackson's brush! This land's big enough for all who want a slice of it.' Suddenly he looked up. 'Anybody heard anything?'

'What kind of thing?' the big man laughed. 'Don't tell me you're getting jittery. It's only the wind in the bushes.'

'I thought I heard . . . ' Smithy stopped and listened again. Then he spat into the fire. 'Oh, to hell! It must be the fire attracting the cats!'

But suddenly he and the others were staring into three muzzles.

'Goddamn! I knew I heard something,' Smithy said disgustedly and raised his hands slowly above his head as the others followed suit.

'Relax, fellers,' Luke da Souza said softly. 'If you do as we say, then you'll keep your skin whole. If you don't, then the widowmaker here will blast you into the great corral in the sky. Right?' He raised his gun slightly and they saw the formidable army issue that he'd used all during the war.

The four men nodded, fascinated by the ugly-looking weapon. The big man's voice wobbled. 'What you want with us, stranger?'

'First, throw down your weapons and Jonas here will look after 'em for you.' Jonas grinned and swept up the guns and tucked them all into his belt. Luke nodded approvingly. 'Now make your way down to the dam. You're going to bend your backs and clear all that debris so that the water runs nice and free as it should do.'

'We'll be missed,' said one of the men hopefully.

'Yes, but not until this job's done and we're long gone.'

'You're mad, mister. Jackson's already preparing to ransack the town and the ranches and when he hears about this, he's gonna take it out of their hides! There'll be a bloodbath!'

For a moment, da Souza hesitated, then realized that nothing would stop Jackson. The folks in the valley would have to rally round and fight for themselves. Meanwhile his plan would go ahead. He shrugged.

'That might well be, mister, but you're going to get stuck in and free this dam, and after that, we're going to give Amos Jackson something else to worry about.'

The men were curious.

'What you mean by that, stranger?'

'Never you mind. Just you get started.' Ferengo and Jonas prodded the men and reluctantly they walked down to the bank of the river, hands still in the air.

Luke surveyed the river. The dam had been strategically placed at its narrowest part.

'Which one of you boys is the strongest swimmer?' he said looking at Ferengo and Jonas. Ferengo raised a mighty arm, well-muscled, that ended in strong shoulders.

'I am, *señor*. I've fought the river in all its moods ever since I could walk.'

'Then you swim over to the other side and keep your gun trained on these two as they work on the dam from that side. Jonas will keep an eye on you fellers on this side and I'll be watching you all and looking out for intruders. If any of your buddies come looking for you, you'll be the first to be shot. So you'd better work fast. Understood?'

Ferengo dived into the water and, with powerful strokes, reached the other side. He dragged himself out of the water and shook himself like a shaggy dog. Then Luke gave the signal and the four men gingerly waded into the fast-running water and two tackled one side of the dam while the other two worked on the nearside.

At first they sweated as the interwoven debris refused to give. Then, suddenly, as dead branches and rotting vegetation disintegrated and were swept away, they could reach down and drag the sodden bags filled with sand and gravel and heave them to one side of the riverbed. Some of the bags burst and the contents were swept away, the momentum of the river itself helping in the task.

It took until dawn for the job to be done. The men climbed out shivering and ready to collapse.

Luke collected wood himself and made a fire and brewed the men's own coffee while they stood steaming in the fire's heat.

'You bastard,' mouthed Smithy. 'We're about all in!'

'Oh, coffee and whatever you've got in your saddle-bags will put new life into you. You'd better eat good, for the next job you're going to do for us will be a real show of strength.'

The men, with Ferengo and Jonas standing over them with their guns, foraged around and brought out bread and dried jerky and they ate their fill.

It was when they were packing away the rest of their gear that Smithy made a play. He had an extra handgun in his saddle-bag and suddenly swivelled around, shooting as he came. One bullet narrowly missed Jonas and the next creased Ferengo's shoulder. He cursed as he clawed for his gun which he'd holstered while they were eating. The men's apparent exhaustion had temporarily put him off guard.

But Luke was ever watchful and plugged Smithy in the heart and the man bounced back against his mount before collapsing. The frightened horse reared into the air and came down hard on the dead man and they all heard the ribs crack.

Then Luke was standing in the low, crouching stance of a professional gunman, looking hard and grim.

'If any of you want to try pulling a trick like that, do it now and we'll get it over with!'

He looked at the three scared weary faces and saw that they were whipped curs.

'Right. Now that we've got that

settled, let's ride. We're going upriver to the fork and then,' — his teeth showed in a wolfish grin — 'you're going to work your butts off building a dam.' He glanced at the dead man. 'A pity we cain't take time to bury this feller. Maybe you boys'll come back later and do the honours?'

The three men's faces brightened.

'So you're not for plugging us and sending us down the river after we do the job?' the big man asked anxiously.

'Nope! My quarrel ain't with you. You do as I say, and do it right, and you're free to go. But I warn you, go back to Jackson and your life is in your own hands. I shoot to kill. No messing!'

The men took their last look at their buddy, Smithy, then the big man collected the dead man's horse and they started their trek upriver. Ferengo led the way with the three prisoners behind him, single file, and Jonas and Luke followed behind.

The river was wider at the fork. They

had moved out of the gorge and the land at each side was flat and sandy. The cliffs of the gorge had dwindled in height to rocky prominences and it was easy to see that the river had divided on itself to work its way along and past the great ridge.

Ferengo watched the three men as Luke and Jonas clambered down to the water's edge to find the best place to build the dam. They were in luck, for a swirl of water had sent dead trees and branches to pile up in a natural barrier at a point where the river swerved. There was also a jumble of rocks to be seen through the clear water. It didn't take much imagination to see how a dam could be built.

Luke looked up at Ferengo and waved.

'Down here! Fetch the men. This is the place.' He stripped off his leather jacket and his shirt and his muscles gleamed in the early morning sun.

Jonas did likewise. It was going to take them all to do the job if they were to succeed. He looked at Luke's back and shoulders and knew that the man was no stranger to hard physical work.

The men were sulky, but when they saw that Luke was willing to work alongside them as were the other men, they worked with a will. They had to, or else they would have frozen in the water that was coming down from the far mountains.

Luke's gun hung at his hip but the men saw he was forever watchful and so, resigned, they worked and suddenly they were taking pride in doing a good job. After all, none of them felt any real loyalty towards Amos Jackson. Why put their lives at risk? Smithy had been a fool. This feller seemed trustworthy. He'd promised they would go free and, somehow, they believed him.

They stopped twice for food and coffee, for now the men were finding it hard to keep up. The huge rocks had to be heaved from their bed in the river and piled into a straggling row across the narrowest part in the fork. It became increasingly hard to struggle against the flow.

The big man, whose name Luke found out, was Jed, was the one who could manhandle the big stuff. He took pride in heaving up a rock three times the size of a man's head as his great muscles swelled and hardened, to drop it with delicate precision just where he wanted it. They found they were working as a team and slowly but surely, they wove a dam of rocks and branches and rotted vegetation that a beaver would have been proud of.

Then they were all standing looking at their finished work, chests heaving, shoulders bowed, as they watched the water hurtle down the left fork and into the gorge and they knew that the water would renew the lifeblood of the valley.

Jed was pensive.

'We cain't go back, boys. If Amos Jackson ever found out we had a hand in this, he'd shoot us down like dogs!'

'Yeah, I was thinking the same thing,' said the smallest man of the three. 'What say if we go back and do right by Smithy, and then light out?'

'Why waste time burying Smithy?' said the third. 'Let's just follow the river upstream and see where it leads.'

'Don't be a fool,' said Jed. 'The river goes back to its source up in the mountains, and where mountains are you find Indians. Besides, winter's coming on and we'd have no chance, even if we didn't run into hostile Indians. No, better go back down into the valley. This feller here, will protect us from the valley folk. We'll go down through the valley south and then where our noses lead us. What say?' He looked at the other two.

They shrugged and agreed.

'Whatever you say, Jed. You're the boss.'

'Then we go and bury Smithy. Is that all right by you, mister?'

'Yep. But you'll have to hurry. I got business with your old boss.'

* * *

Amos Jackson was spitting fire.

'Where the hell are those men? They should have been back last night! Don't tell me they weren't ready to come back. Nobody wants to do a double shift if they don't have to, unless, of course, they wanted to get out of going on this raid.'

He looked around at the waiting men all set to ride. None of them looked enthusiastic. They were a bunch of yellow-bellied shysters, ready to take a man's wages, but not ready to work for their dough, he raged inwardly. He blamed his sons. If they'd shown the same ruthlessness as himself it would have rubbed off on the others. But if the boss's sons snivelled what else could you expect from the men?

'We cain't wait any longer,' he bellowed. 'We've got a lot of riding to do. Did you all make free with that whiskey at breakfast time?'

'Yeh, yeh, yeh!' there were some

enthusiastic shouts from those who'd made more than free. 'Don't worry,' a voice in the crowd shouted, 'we're all tanked up to do what we have to do. Yes sir!' There were ragged cheers and laughter and one man got excited and took a shot at a passing bird.

'None of that,' roared Amos. 'Keep your bullets for those intended for them. We're going all out today to bring those valley folk to heel. I want them on the way out of the valley by nightfall. If we do the trick, then it's bonuses all round. Now, let's ride!'

The cavalcade forded the river and rode for Sweetwater Butte ignoring the small farms they passed. They would be dealt with later. There were those working in the fields who straightened their backs and watched the bunch of riders pass by.

Tim O'Leary looked at his wife and put an arm about her.

'I don't like it, Mary. Why would Jackson bring all his men to this side of the river and ride so hard towards the town?'

She looked up at him.

'You think there's mischief afoot?'

'I do.'

'Then there's only one thing you can do, Tim. You've got to go and warn Mr Schofield. He's got the men to do something about it.'

'But that would mean leaving you and the kids alone!'

She looked at him bravely.

'You've got to do it, Tim. If they cause mayhem in the town, and are successful, they could come back and sack all the farms.'

Tim nodded and rubbed his hairy chin.

'If I rode the old nag hard, I could be there in three hours.'

'You do it, Tim, and while you're saddling up I'll make you a beef sandwich to have on the way.'

'Sure, you're a good lass, Mary.' He gave her an extra hug, then strode away to saddle up his old horse.

Amos Jackson halted the headlong gallop by raising a hand. The men clustered behind him, all looking down the hill to the straggling town nestling in the bottom of the valley.

It was all hustle and bustle in the main street. There was a wagon outside the food store and a man, whom Amos recognized as one of the dirt farmers, was humping a sack of flour and heaving it aboard.

There were women walking the sidewalks, stopping to chat with each other, and the blacksmith was leading a horse into the smithy while its owner clapped it on the rump.

There were several horses tied to the hitching rail before the saloon and the undertaker was to be seen supervising the loading of a coffin on to a black hearse that had glass sides.

Amos wondered if he knew the deceased. He smiled grimly. The undertaker was going to be busy during the next few hours, that is if he was sensible and didn't join the fight.

Mark rode up beside him, his face worried.

'Pa, there's time to have second thoughts . . . ' Amos turned savagely towards him.

'And lose the respect of the men? Don't be a fool! I'm going to own this valley, one way or another. I've offered to buy them all out and they laughed at me! Now I'm going to take!'

'But Pa . . . '

Amos leaned over and caught Mark a stinging blow on his cheek.

'Get back with the others! You're no son of mine! I was right all along. Your mother was a whore!' Mark, sick at heart because of the coming fight, grew angry at the slur on his dead mother. He knew what he must do and he would do it!

He rowelled his horse, turned and joined Hank, his face black with fury.

'What did he say?' asked Hank. 'We all saw him hit you.'

Mark's lips tightened.

'I'll kill the bastard!'

'Mark!' Hank sounded horrified. Mark looked at him.

'You're the youngest and you hardly remember Ma. He called her a whore,' he said bitterly, 'and I can't forgive him for that. She was the best ma a man could have. He beat her to death!'

They moved on, a little behind the rest. Hank looked worried.

'You really mean to kill him?'

'Wouldn't you, if he insulted and humiliated you in front of the men? And if you'd known our ma as I did? I'll not shoot him in the back though. I'll face him and tell him what a bastard he is and look him in the eyes . . . '

'He'll kill you! He's ruthless. He'll do it while you're thinking about it!'

'Hank, I don't much care any more. I'm sick to my soul and I swear I'll not lift my gun to those folk down in the valley. What about you?'

'I'll do as you do. I've got no guts

for this. All I want is a peaceful life.'

'And we won't get it until Pa is six feet under!'

The riders increased their speed and now were passing straggling wagons coming into town. They created a whirlwind of dust. As they entered town, Amos rode ahead and the men spread out behind him. They galloped down Main Street, scattering all before them. Guns pointed into the air and shots mingled with the screams of women as they fled into doorways.

Kurt Schmidt from the drugstore came out to see what all the fuss was about. He caught a bullet in the shoulder and fell to the ground as the barber peered out of his window with a shotgun cocked. He never got to use it, as the glass from his window shattered and a long, pointed shard stuck in his throat.

The horsemen came to a halt outside the dry goods store and, as the excited horses pranced and snorted, Amos Jackson said tersely to one of his men, 'Right, Chet, you know what to do, do it!'

Chet brought out a greasewood torch, the end wrapped in rags already soaked in oil. The men around him sat poised, guns aimed on the awed townsfolk caught before they could run. They all watched as Chet lit the torch with a lucifer and then flung it into the store.

There was a yell and the storekeeper and several customers ran out. The men outside hustled them away. The storekeeper's eyes were bolting from his head.

'Get back! Get back!' he screamed. 'That goddamn torch landed on a barrel of gunpowder! The whole damn place will go up in a minute!'

There was the crackle of flames, then the earsplitting explosion and the storefront erupted in a showering mass of wood and glass.

But now the riders were galloping up and down the street, shooting up anything that moved. The whiskey was working and when the men drinking in the saloon poured out with guns blazing, they were ready for them and cut them down before the drinkers knew what it was all about.

Mark and Hank rode up and down the street firing into the air and trying to warn those who would listen.

Then the townsfolk got their second wind and began to fight back. Old shotguns and army rifles came out and even the owner of the women's dress shop opened up and blazed away with her father's old gun.

Suddenly there were still bodies lying in the street and riderless horses galloping crazily, reins flapping and crashing into riders who were now in the throes of bloodlust.

Several of Jackson's men had raided the saloon and Sam was down on the ground with a growing stain of red covering his chest. The men were swigging from bottles and two of them rushed upstairs to find the women and brought them down at gunpoint.

There were catcalls and whooping as the woman-starved men stared at the girls in every state of undress. Some were in white linen basques and bloomers, others showing legs in black stockings and fancy garters and little else.

The men goggled and the girls bunched together, crossing arms over pink-tipped bosoms and looking frightened. This was very different to entertaining a man on her home ground which was her bedroom. There, she was in charge; here, she was just one of a herd of women who were being looked over as if they were lumps of meat.

Then a huge ox of a man made a grab for a girl with red hair and that was a signal for the rest to rush forward to claim one.

They were pushed and poked and their tender flesh bruised, but they fought back with long fingernails and teeth that bit into a man's flesh.

But, as a man subdued and claimed a woman, there was another man ready to wrest her away from him. They came to blows and soon the saloon was a mass of fighting men. The girls crawled away to escape into the kitchen at the back of the saloon and then outside into the yard where the privy was beside the pigpens.

They barricaded themselves into a pigpen despite an irate mother of eight young piglets. They would rather brave a savage mother than take on the wild Jackson crew crazed with woman lust.

Further down the street, other fires raged as the wind blew sparks from the burning store which ignited dry wooden buildings. Soon, there was a wall of fire running down the street, flames licking upwards of thirty feet. Townsfolk came out screaming, some burdened with treasures they wanted to save. Others carried babies, dragging children behind them and one old lady tried to drag a wooden chest behind her, crying to anyone who would listen that it contained her wedding dress. Nobody stopped to help her and she struggled until she fell down with her arms protectively around her chest. She lay in the road defenceless, gasping and sobbing, until a horse's hoof kicked her in the head and she lay still.

Amos Jackson, wild and exultant, with the mad light of triumph in his eyes, urged the men on as he rode up and down the main street. Then his eyes lit on his son, Hank, who was assisting the middle-aged schoolmarm, Miss Bentley, to carry books out of the burning school. She was sobbing as she staggered under a pile of books too heavy for her. Hank was also burdened and so, when his father confronted him, Hank was helpless.

'What the hell do you think you're doing?' raved the old man. 'You're not supposed to help these folk, you're supposed to drive them out!'

Miss Bentley stared at him over the top of her books, both contempt and rage in her eyes.

'May you rot in hell, Amos Jackson! Your son is twice the man you are!

You're nothing but a crawling, slimy, dung-eating beetle! You're an insult to the human race and I hope you suffer all the pains of Hell before you die!'

'Why you goddamned, arrogant bitch; you'll suffer Hell's pains first!' He shot her in the forehead and her blood spilled over her beloved books before they cascaded on to the ground as she collapsed in a heap.

Hank threw down his load of books and reached for his gun.

'She was right, Pa, you *are* a slimy, dung-eating beetle. My biggest hope in life is that I'm not your son!' With that he aimed at his father's heart, but before he could pull the trigger his father's bullet had taken him down.

Amos stared at him. There was no remorse or compassion in him.

'You never were my son, Hank. Only Abe was my true son. You, Ned and Mark were your mother's sons, whoever your father was.' He rode on and never looked back.

★ ★ ★

Morton Schofield with his boys and the rounded-up dirt farmers, bunched together as they paused to blow their horses before riding down into town.

They could see the black pall of smoke and the orange glow of flames as the fire in Sweetwater Butte took hold. The sound of shots came faintly on the wind.

'Goddamnit! We're going to be too late,' bawled Schofield into Tim O'Leary's ear. 'The whole town's being destroyed!'

'But to be sure we'll not be too late to take on Jackson and his mob. If we don't, then we can say goodbye to all we've worked for. Let's go get 'em!' Tim O'Leary dug his heels into his horse's ribs and set off at a gallop downhill and the rest followed.

Far up the side of the valley along the forest line, Luke da Souza and the two half-breeds watched the bunch of men riding down at breakneck speed towards the town. They saw the devastation there and the man from Socorro's eyes were cold and determined.

'I want to get the Jacksons before that mob take them. I want the man who killed my brother!'

The three men sent their horses at a gallop down the steep gradient into the valley below, sparks flying as hooves slipped on hard rock and then later, creating a dustcloud, as their madlong gallop brought them to the edge of the town.

They beat the oncoming posse by only minutes, but it was enough for Luke to race down the street hunting for the Jackson brothers. Ferengo and Jonas guarded his back but it was hardly necessary for now victory had gone to the head of the Jackson crew and they were looting the houses that had not been fired. The townsfolk had fled, leaving smoking homes that were now just charred wood.

Some of the people had chosen to stay and had barricaded themselves into their homes. Now the looters were concentrating on dragging them out after threats of firing the shacks. So it was with panic that the looters watched the charging posse gallop into town, guns blazing, horses rearing and ropes swinging. Many of the men tried to flee, but were too drunk to run.

Then came the horrendous sight of men hauled along the ground, bumping and scraping until clothing and skin was ripped away and only the raw redness of bloody meat remained.

The ranchers were taking their revenge. The lucky ones were strung up and lynched, several to a tree, and left to swing in the wind.

Mark Jackson watched with horror. His terror caught in his throat. This was all because of his father's obsession of claiming the valley as his own. He turned to look for Amos. He would kill him and then kill himself.

Instead, he came face to face with Luke da Souza, and a worse dread turned his guts to water.

Luke's lariat snaked out and curled around him, and he was dragged away from the mêlée going on and into a yard behind the ruined blacksmith's shop.

Then Luke dismounted and cut him free.

'What you want with me . . . Major?'

'So you recognize me, Jackson. I want to know about your brother, Abe. I want to know who contacted him and why he turned spy.'

'I don't know. Abe did things my brothers and I didn't approve of.'

'But you knew he was spying?'

'Yes. Ned caught him at it and he went along with it. Abe was flashing Yankee money around. Said Confederate money would be no good after the war and that we'd all be ruined. He said Pa . . . ' He stopped abruptly and tightened his lips.

'Yes, what about your pa?'

'I don't remember.'

Luke shot between his feet and the dust flew. Mark did a little war-dance.

'You'd better remember, or next time I'll aim higher.'

'For the love of God, if you're going to kill me, get on and do it and stop playing cat and mouse!'

'You're no good dead. I want the man who persuaded Abe to work for the Yankees.'

Mark wet his lips and watched Luke da Souza's gunhand. He took a deep breath.

'If I tell you will you let me go?'

Luke laughed. 'You've got some gall, mister. Let's just say that your passing could be easy or it could be hard. It's your choice. I also want to know which of you boys bushwhacked my brother and I after Petersburg.'

Mark swallowed again. 'Does it matter? He was killed and I'm going to die, anyway.'

'I'd just like to know.'

'Then you need look no further. I shot you both! I did it for Ned, not for Abe. He was a bastard, but Ned was the one who protected us younger ones against our father. He didn't deserve to lose an arm. He's a good man is Ned.'

Luke nodded.

'I guessed it would be you. That younger brother of yours hadn't the spunk. He was a dreamer. Couldn't even take orders properly in battle.'

Mark listened with his head down. Suddenly he lifted his head.

'I'll make it easy for you,' he said and dived for his gun, but before it was out of its holster, Luke's bullet caught him in the chest.

'Goddamn!' Luke knelt beside the body. Mark's eyes fluttered and his lips stretched into something like a smile.

'You want . . . to know . . . '

'Yes,' whispered Luke. 'Who was it made Abe a traitor?'

'My . . . my . . . father. May . . . his soul . . . roast . . . in Hell!' Mark choked as the blood poured from his mouth.

Luke stood upright. So he'd been right and for once, General Lee had been wrong. No wonder the defences at Petersburg had collapsed with men like Amos Jackson infiltrating the Confederate Army by sending their sons to war and turning them into spies.

It was said that Amos Jackson had been against his sons joining up, but it had all been camouflage. Abe, the eldest, had been in his father's confidence; no doubt Amos reckoned his other sons were not to be trusted.

Anger seethed through Luke. How much harm and how much death had Amos Jackson been responsible for? He thought of his dead brother and the two Jackson brothers, all dead because of Amos Jackson and his crazy obsession with money and power.

There was such hate in Luke at that moment, it sent him momentarily crazy. He wanted to get his hands about the bastard's neck and watch his eyes bulge as he choked to death.

'I'll find that bastard, and when I do,' he said between clenched teeth, 'he'll wish he'd been caught by the Apaches!'

5

Amos Jackson watched the burning buildings with a mad exultation. This was what he wanted, the total annihilation of Sweetwater Butte so that he could take over the whole valley. He wanted a ghost town, burned down to the very bedrock. He cared nothing for the good folk who'd spent their lives building up a community that believed in helping each other during bad times.

This spirit of oneness had been forged during early Indian raids when the only way to survive was to band together. There had been no need for the law in Sweetwater Butte. There was no sheriff and no jail. A picked band of the elders of the town had run it and all had been well until Amos Jackson had gathered about him the experienced and disillusioned survivors of the War

Between the States. They, for the most part had no homes to go back to, were ambitious and mercenary. They held no loyalty for anyone but themselves.

Now he watched those men turn to wolves, go wild and loot and burn as if they were once more fighting a war.

It frightened him. Made him uneasy. He wanted the death of the town, but he didn't want those men turning on him. Goddammit! They were getting out of hand! Anyone trying to stop them would be shot. There was an ugly menace in the air, a buzzing as if some long sleeping creature was awake and planning evil.

The fantasy was rudely shattered when big Art, riding a horse much too small for him, rode up, eyes wild and smelling of fear.

'There's a posse coming down the road, boss, and it looks mighty like Morton Schofield's leading it.'

'A posse?'

'Yeah, and it's a big 'un. I reckon Schofield's got all the dirt farmers with him! We'll have to get out of here!'

Amos licked his lips. He was no general. His genius was to order others, not fight battles, or plan tactics. He made up his mind in a moment.

'Yes, we'll have to get out. Round up as many men as you can and we'll ride south towards Lacey's place and ford the river lower down. Don't wait about. If you can't get all the men, leave 'em. They'll have to fend for themselves!'

'Yes, boss.' Art galloped off, rolling from side to side, his bulk making him clumsy.

It took a while to round up the men and in that time Amos saw for himself the cloud of dust coming at great speed along the dirt road into town He cursed. Damn Morton Schofield! It would have been better to sack his place first before descending on the town.

Then Art was back with a tattered rabble, who were more drunk than sober and who whistled and gave wild

111

Rebel yells as they galloped out of the burning town.

Out of town, Amos pulled up and turned watching the mayhem they had caused.

'Where the hell's Mark?' he yelled at a sweating Art.

'Didn't see hair or hide of him back there. Could be already hiding out.' Art gave him a sly look and Amos wasn't slow to catch his drift.

It figured. There had only been one son like himself. The rest had all been yellow-livered. It hurt to think of Abe, but the others could go to hell.

He hardened his jaw and dug his heels into his horse. What had he to grieve about? He vented his anger on the major. If he hadn't returned, he would have had nothing to worry about.

But he would have his revenge on this goddamned Major Luke da Souza. He would have to think about it. It would have to be something special and it would have to be out at the ranch, where he could take his time and make the bastard suffer.

The answer came as they rode south towards the end of the valley. They rode smack into John Lacey and his bunch of half-breed riders, and with them was John Lacey's daughter.

Amos Jackson's mind worked fast. He guessed that da Souza was a man who would always respond to a woman in trouble, for he'd been an officer, therefore he must be a gentleman.

Art looked at him and then at the advancing party.

'What we do now, boss?'

'They're enemies, aren't they?' He turned and waved his arm at his men. 'Go get 'em, boys, but I want the girl!'

The men shrieked and howled and charged at the surprised party, guns spitting and the dust rising as the skirmish moved savagely into a massacre.

John Lacey tried to lead his daughter's horse out of the fray and took a bullet in the shoulder. He threw her the leading rein.

'Ride like hell, love, and get into those trees, then make for the village.' He coughed and, as she watched, wide-eyed, he slumped in the saddle as another slug took him in the chest.

Panic hit her and she dug her heels into her horse and left the milling men at a gallop. She tore through small trees and scrub, bruising her face and shoulders against whipping branches. Then, just as she thought she was clear away, a whistling rope landed around the horse's neck pulling it up so abruptly she took a header on to the hard ground.

She lay, half stunned, looking up at a grinning Art.

'The boss wants you. What for, I don't know. He's an old man, so it cain't be your body he's after!' He grinned again as if he'd made a great joke.

Then she was being hauled to her feet and lifted roughly on to her mount, but this time her feet were tied under the horse's belly and her hands tied tightly to the pommel. It was uncomfortable and she was frightened.

They cut across country and were waiting at the ford near her father's land when the rest of the party joined them.

The men were quiet now the blood-lust left them. They looked at each other sideways as they remembered the scene of the massacre. Some of the men had known John Lacey and liked him. Now they could not meet the girl's scornful eyes.

'Murderers! I hope you all burn in Hell!' she spat at them. 'And as for you' — she looked Amos Jackson up and down — 'I hope your entrails burn and you die inch by inch! Shooting would be too quick for you!'

'Careful, honey. Just remember who's boss around here. A nod of the head and any one of these men would take you out and' — he smiled — 'play with you before killing you in any way he pleased. So watch your step.'

'It would have to be someone else,

wouldn't it? You wouldn't have the stomach to kill me yourself!' she goaded, despite her fear.

He frowned.

'I don't want you dead. You're bait, m'dear. I'm sending a messenger to da Souza. I doubt whether he will leave you in my hands. He'll want to play the gallant and save the damsel in distress!' He smiled. 'You see, I've read a few books in my time. I know how young men react when a woman is in danger.'

Gradually they travelled to higher ground. The trail left the valley which Marie-Anne observed was in better condition than at the other side of Snake River. The cattle that grazed were fatter. The grass, although brown was much thicker and longer than the scrubby stuff on the other side.

She set her teeth. Now she knew why. She'd heard her father talking heatedly about Jackson's unneighbourly actions in damming the river where it forked and separated. It was a deliberate ploy to ruin a whole community. She remembered Miss Bentley's lectures on tyrants through the ages. Now she was meeting one face to face.

'You won't get away with this,' she mumbled, as they pushed ahead, and he, riding by her side, laughed. 'All tyrants overreach themselves in time. Miss Bentley told us so. Power goes to a tyrant's head and he makes mistakes . . . '

'Shut up and be quiet! That Miss Bentley of yours was talking out of the back of her head! If a man has the guts and the know-how, he can do anything he likes!' Then as an afterthought he said casually, 'Being what she was, didn't do your Miss Bentley any good. She died down there, you know, protecting a load of old books!'

Marie-Anne looked at him with horror and shock. Love for Miss Bentley brought pain and she reached across and struck him on the cheek.

'Pig! May God never forgive you for

what you've done to her and all those good folk of the valley! Your name will stink in the nostrils of all good men . . . '

A resounding blow to her head would have knocked her off the horse if she hadn't been tied down. As it was, she swayed, twisting her back agonizingly so that she cried out sharply.

'I said, be quiet, you shrewish bitch! Another word from you and I'll have you gagged.' Then Amos motioned to big Art to come up beside him. 'Take her back amongst the men and guard her well. I'm sick of listening to the high-and-mighty bitch. She's got a tongue like a razor!'

Art took the reins and dropped back with Marie-Anne. The band of men surrounded her and she was subjected to their coarse remarks and mocking laughter.

'You're all drunk and behaving worse than animals,' she said cuttingly, 'and I hope you all hang!' She set her teeth and stared ahead, willing herself not to listen to their jeering remarks.

'Hoity-toity, isn't she, fellers?'

'Wait until Jackson gets da Souza in his sights! Then we'll show her what real men can do!'

'Not so hoity-toity then!'

'We'll put her up for auction!'

'Nah! We'll play poker for her and all drink at the well!'

Marie-Anne rode staring straight ahead, trying to cut out the remarks, but inwardly she was shaking with fear. These men were worse than Indians, because they were white. If she'd had a gun she would have shot herself . . .

They came at last into the yard and Marie-Anne was lifted not ungently from the saddle after her thongs were loosed. Her legs were like jelly and the pain as the blood started circulating was nearly more than she could bear.

Art caught and held her and finally carried her into the ranch and deposited her roughly on a wooden settle.

'What you want done with her, boss?' Art asked.

'Oh, tie her to a chair,' Amos replied indifferently. 'I wonder where the hell Ned is? Avoiding me as usual, I suppose.' He strode off to the veranda and, as the remainder of his men unsaddled and led their horses away, he counted them. He was bitter. There were at least eight men missing. His venom turned itself on to his son. 'Ned, you skulking bastard! Where the hell are you?' His voice echoed across the yard and beyond.

Ned, tending to a newly born foal as best he could with one hand, rose to his feet, watching the foal stagger its first few steps to the mare who was trembling and sniffing at its young.

'Easy, girl, it's your first so don't tread on it. You've got a fine colt and you deserve the best.' He bunched clean straw around them both. The stable, well away from the other buildings was his idea, for sometimes mares had difficult births. Several times Ned had saved an otherwise still-birth.

He loved horses. All the love that was

in him was channelled to his horses. They compensated for lack of a father's love. There was no woman in his life, for the life they led on the ranch didn't encourage the meeting of women and he couldn't bear the thought of going to a whorehouse and being laughed at for being a one-armed cripple.

The only women he'd experienced had been those who'd followed the army. They had been so bold that they'd intimidated him as a shy green youth. So, when he thought of women, he thought of those hard-faced harpies and shuddered. Horses, he realized, gave you love and no complications and, when his stallion, Blackstone, served a mare and she gave birth to a healthy foal, then he was truly proud and happy.

Life would be perfect if his father wasn't around.

He heard his father's stentorian call. He'd known something was afoot, but as usual he was not in his father's confidence and he'd watched them ride out at dawn with little curiosity. He saw Mark and Hank head the posse with their father and shrugged. If those two fools went along with their father's mad ideas, then so be it. One of these days, he would gather up his herd of horses and move out. It would take courage and determination to do it, and that was what he lacked. He despised himself for it.

Now, he leaned his head against the rough wooden door of the stable. There was something in the old man's tone that sent icy fingers up his back. The mad bastard was about to blow.

He dreaded his father's rages. One never knew what to expect. One of these days his father would push him too far and he'd kill the goddamned swine.

He crossed the yard reluctantly, seeing the irate figure on the veranda steps.

'What the hell have you been doing? You should have been here when we rode in. What kept you?'

'I've been birthing a foal. The mother needed attention.'

Amos spat at his feet.

'You and your blasted horses! One of these days I'm going to ship out all that pampered pedigree stock of yours and you can make do with our working horses. They're eating good grub and the herd gets bigger every year!'

'If you did that I'd be leaving,' growled Ned. Amos looked hard at him.

'I don't believe you! You haven't got the guts!'

Ned reddened with fury, because, up until now, his father was right. He should have got out when he came home from the war and realized that his father couldn't bear to look at him.

But before he could make an angry retort, Amos surprised him.

'You can put the thought of leaving me right out of your head. I need you, Ned, as I never did before!' Ned swallowed. He was angry, bewildered

123

and out of his depth.

'You've never said that before!'

'No. I never thought I ever should. But you're all I have left now, Ned. Your brothers are dead. Murdered by those bastards over the river!' he lied, refusing to remember Hank's death at his own hands.

'Not murdered by them, Pa! Murdered because of you! You're to blame!' Ned, eyes blazing, gutted with the pain of losing his brothers in such a senseless fashion, lunged at his father and drove his fist into the old man's jaw.

He staggered and fell and Ned straddled him and kept punching with his one fist until big Art coming across the yard ran and dragged him off.

Art held him fast as the old man dragged himself to his feet. Ned breathed heavily, a red mist of rage still before his eyes.

'What's going on, boss?' Art still held Ned although Ned had ceased to struggle.

'Let him go,' Amos said wearily. 'I told him about Mark and Hank and he blamed me.' Amos, his head down, walked into the ranch house, suddenly haunted by the remembered look in Hank's eyes.

Art looked at Ned. 'You all right, son?'

Ned nodded. 'I'm fine.'

'You'll not do anything foolish? A man doesn't kill his pa.'

Ned gave him a twisted grin.

'Pa always maintained he wasn't our pa, only Abe's. If I kill him it would be no great crime. Right?'

Art looked concerned.

'Better keep out of his way for a few days. Another thing, there's a girl in there.' He nodded inside the open door. 'Someone's going to have to watch her.'

'What we doing with a girl here?' Ned was amazed. This was an all-male establishment.

'It's the Lacey girl. Your pa figures that da Souza will come running when he hears about it.'

'You mean he kidnapped her?'

'Yeah, you might say that. I reckon your pa has just blown his lid, but it might just come off. The town's razed to the ground. We left it burning.' Art was in fear and awe at Amos Jackson's determination and willpower. 'The old man sure got the boys going! They got wild and drunk and really let 'em have it! It was like the Battle of Fredericksburg all over again!'

'What about the ranchers and farmers?'

Art scowled. 'Morton Schofield brought a posse into town with all the rabble he could muster, and that was when we lost our men. Some of them stopped to fight but your pa said to back off and that's what saved us. Your pa's a good general, even though he is a bit touched, up aloft!'

'So we can expect an attack?'

'If Schofield has the balls for it, but I doubt it. None of them were military men. They stayed home and got on with making a life for themselves. Your pa was the one who took us ex-army dropouts to work for him. We're the ones who can turn the Sweetwater Valley into one huge ranch, and we're going to do it!'

Ned balled his fist at the big man's arrogance. He'd never liked Art for several reasons; he was coarse and bullying, he was a toady to his father and had gotten him and his brothers into more grief than they might have done; and he made Ned feel like a puny teenager and now, after losing an arm, he knew he was the subject of overt jokes.

Now he was being insufferable as if he was the old man's number one lieutenant.

'Ned! Get yourself back here, damn you!' His father's shout wasn't as forceful as usual. He'd shaken the bastard when he'd gone for him. It felt good to let the old man know how he really felt about him. Ned straightened his back and stared at Art.

'I'd better go and see what the old devil wants!'

Art laughed. 'Yeah, you do that. Maybe he wants you to nursemaid the girl. I suppose you're up to that?' He walked away, his big shoulders heaving as he chuckled to himself.

Ned slowly stepped into the living-room. He hated himself for not acting bold. But it wasn't his nature. His eyes sought his father's and then passed on to the girl tied to the chair.

He recognized her. She hadn't changed from the kid he'd seen coming out of the schoolhouse all those years ago. She'd had a sweet smile then. Now she glared at him.

'What you want?' he asked gruffly. His father looked shaken.

'Think you can guard this girl while I supervise the boys?'

Art was right, damn him! He was being relegated to nursemaid as if that was all he was good for. He stared at the girl. Maybe it wouldn't be such a bad job after all. At least they could talk.

'I reckon.'

'Good. You'd better get Cookie rustle something up for her. It was a long haul for a girl. Oh, and Ned . . .'

'Yes, Pa?'

'Don't loosen her up too much. Just enough for her to eat. Right?'

'Yes, Pa.'

The old man lumbered out stiffly. There had been no more cursing because he'd knocked him down. Ned marvelled. Maybe he should have asserted himself years ago! Maybe all of them should. He remembered Abe and how he had never let his father have the last word. He'd been the wild one and Pa had thought the sun shone out of his ass. Too late for Hank and Mark. He wondered what arrangements his father was making to recover the bodies.

Surely he wouldn't leave them to be disposed of by strangers?

'What you staring at?' The girl's voice penetrated his thoughts. Startled, he looked at her. 'You heard that goddamned father of yours. I could do with a drink and I sure could eat something.'

'I'll see Cookie.'

'I could use the privy too.'

'Ah . . . ' His father never said anything about the privy. He looked doubtfully at her. 'You'll have to wait.'

'Not too long I hope.'

He bit his lip. He wasn't used to womenfolk, not respectable women.

'I'd have to go with you. There's no women here to watch you. I'm sorry.'

'You're not like your father, are you? Your father and my father used to be friendly neighbours in the old days. I remember you as a tall gawky boy with big eyes. I always thought you couldn't speak.'

He gave a wry smile. 'I was frightened of girls, even little girls. As a matter of fact, I still am!' He was startled at his admission, but somehow it was important not to be like his father.

'Poor you. Do you think I could have

130

a drink now? My tongue is parched.'

'Yes, certainly.' He hastened away to the cookhouse and gave Cookie orders to rustle up some grub and give him a clean mug with newly made coffee.

While he was gone, Marie-Anne wrestled with her bonds, but those at her ankles were tight and her wrist bonds only bit more as she struggled.

He held the mug to her lips, but it was too hot. She jumped.

'For God's sake, loosen these ropes! I'm not going anywhere, am I?' She glared at him in temper.

She fascinated him. She was like an unbroken colt. She had what he lacked, that spirit of defiance that would not give in to browbeating. Without a word, he cut her ropes and gave her the mug of coffee.

'Here, take it. As you say, you're going nowhere.'

Cookie brought her a bowl of warmed up beef stew, and a hunk of bread and Ned watched her eat ravenously and not like a lady.

Then she looked at him squarely in the eye.

'You're going to have to let me go to the privy or I'll go all over the floor.'

Ned gulped. This was no lady talking. She sounded like one of the hands. Chre-ist! What should he do? She laughed deep in her throat.

'Got a problem, have you, Ned Jackson? Cain't make your mind up without your pa's sayso?' she goaded.

He flushed. Damn her!

'I don't have to have Pa's permission to breathe,' he said hotly.

'Then think for yourself. Do you want me sitting in my own filth?' He flushed again but this time it wasn't embarrassment but at a certain arousal in himself. God! She was some woman!

He knelt at her feet without saying a word, and drew back her skirt and petticoats and saw her shapely legs clad in black cotton. There was a hint of white linen drawers just below the knee. His hands trembled as he cut the ropes that bound her ankles.

Then he was standing and clasping her arm so that she could stand and the warmth of her soft flesh sent currents rushing through him.

'It's at the end of the yard. I'll take you there.' He could hardly mouth the words.

He walked stiffly by her side until they reached the small wooden building and she stepped inside. He waited, leaning against the rough plank door.

Then the latch was lifted and she came out, but, too late, he remembered the shovel that was kept to clean out the privy when it was overflowing. It hit him with all the muscle Marie-Anne could bring to bear.

'I'm sorry, Ned,' she said between her teeth. 'You're nothing like your pa, but what has to be done has to be!' Then she was out running as fast as her lifted skirts would allow to the corral where the horses were tied ready to ride.

She mounted quickly, closed her eyes

and took the fence at a lunge. The horse buckled and nearly came down but a mighty pull on the reins brought his head up and he regained his stride. Then, hair flying wild, she took off downhill towards the river. There were no shouts of alarm: she'd got away.

But that state of affairs didn't last long. A man on lookout saw the lone rider racing across the scrubby grass. He galloped into the yard and demanded to see Amos who was in the bunkhouse giving out orders. Amos Jackson came out to see what the commotion was all about.

'Hal, what are you doing here? You're supposed to be on lookout on Beacon Hill.'

'Your prisoner's escaped, boss. I've just seen a woman riding hell for leather down towards the river!'

'The hell you have! If you're right, I'll string that sonofabitch up!' He strode off to the main house shouting as he went. 'Ned! Are you there?

What's this about . . . ' He stopped
as he stepped inside and saw the cut
ropes. 'Goddammit! The little yellow-
bellied slimeball's let her go!'

He stormed through the house and
saw the open back door and went into
the yard and looked at the crumpled
mass that was his son. He kicked him
in the ribs.

'Ned! I'll have your balls for this!'
Then he bent over him and saw the
huge bump on the head. He looked
around and noted the open privy door
and the privy shovel lying close by.
'So she diddled you, hey? You stupid,
misbegotten toad!' He dragged him up
and shook him. Ned opened his eyes
and blinked.

'She hit me, Pa! I forgot about the
shovel.'

'You stupid idiot! I was a fool to
expect you could do a simple job like
watching a roped up woman!'

'What was I supposed to do? She
wanted the privy!'

'You should have made her wait, or

crap herself. What odds?'

He slapped Ned on both cheeks and then stalked off, leaving Ned sobbing and in a cold rage. He would definitely kill that crazy old man some day!

6

Luke da Souza and the two half-breeds pushed their way through the tall scrub, leading their horses and protecting themselves from whipping branches, cursing as they did so. They had ridden up and around the Jackson ranch coming towards it from the rear.

They moved cautiously, closing in only after careful surveillance, looking out for guards or anything untoward underfoot.

Luke da Souza groped for his glasses. Something was happening at the ranch; there was much coming and going. As he watched, old man Jackson himself, stood on the veranda, waving his arms and shouting.

Something had gone wrong which hadn't pleased Amos. Da Souza gritted his teeth at the sight of him. He was the father of the traitor he'd shot dead and all the evidence was that this old man was the instigator, who'd manipulated his oldest son to betray the Rebel cause, and in doing so had also been responsible for the crippling of his son, Ned.

Luke wasn't gunning for Ned. That poor devil had just been caught up in his father's and brother's machinations. He doubted if Ned and the younger Jacksons had ever been party to the betrayal. But they were all Jacksons and, to the army, they were all tarred with the same brush.

Now, all Luke da Souza wanted was to make Amos Jackson pay for the death of his own brother, Ed, and the betrayal of Petersburg and the deaths of many of the comrades who'd ridden shoulder to shoulder with the Jackson brothers.

There was also the girl and the death of John Lacey, who'd saved his life, to consider. It was his duty to bring her back to the safety of the Lacey ranch. It was now hers. Small it might be as ranches went, but it was the only home she'd ever known.

He thought, too, of the devastation in the quiet backwater town called Sweetwater Butte. Amos Jackson had a lot to answer for.

Now he watched the tall stooped figure. He wished he'd been near enough to put a bullet in his forehead. He turned to the two watching men.

'We'll leave the horses and make our way to the corral and use the horses as cover. We'll locate the girl . . . ' Then he stopped to curse as a rider with flying skirts crouched low and leapt over the corral fence.

From far above, she was just a tiny moving dot, but his glasses picked out her flying hair and strained white face as she galloped madly downwards at breakneck speed towards the river.

'There she goes!' shouted Luke. 'By God, the girl has courage!'

For a long moment they watched her progress and then they saw the lone rider gallop madly to the ranch. It was time to take a hand.

Without waiting for orders, Ferengo and Jonas were already forking their mounts. Luke followed suit and they cut across country and downhill as fast as their horses could travel.

Ferengo and Jonas had known Marie-Anne Lacey since she was a small child. They had dandled her on their knees and played with her and held her on her first pony. Now, they rode like avenging angels, ready to protect her with their lives.

They were closing in on her and she looked back and saw them coming, but, frightened at seeing three riders so nearly upon her and, in the far distance, other riders coming spickety-lick downhill after her, she spurred her horse to greater efforts and tore into the thorn bushes that grew near the riverbank.

She turned north and followed the river, dodging thorny pears, overgrown water reeds, braving clouds of disturbed insects as she went.

She heard shouts behind her, but was too panicked to listen. All she wanted was to get away. She was moving into territory she'd never been in before. She knew the river cut through the valley at its head and beyond that were the mountains from which the river sprang.

She knew she should have turned south towards home, but there had been no cover and she was determined that the horrible Jackson men shouldn't capture her alive.

She was sobbing. Sweat trickled down her face and small insects, attracted by the saltiness, clung to her skin. Her long hair was in lank wisps and bits of foliage were enmeshed within it. There was blood on the horse, where it had forced its way through thorns. It also limped and she could feel it tremble under her at each step.

Dear God, help me, she prayed as she pressed on. Already she was thirsty, but dared not stop to find a place by

141

the river where she and the horse might drink.

The lamed horse was reduced to a walk. Its head hung low and because she loved horses, she dismounted and, taking the bridle, led the beast.

She stumbled and fell over an exposed tree root and the horse stood swishing its tail as she dragged herself upright. She laid her head on the horse's sweating side and cried, the smell of horse sweat strong in her nostrils.

Then suddenly she was aware of a crashing coming through the brush. Her head came up like that of a startled deer and she listened. She heard a man's voice and he was calling, 'Marie-Anne!' Or was it some kind of delirious dream?

The voice came again and again, nearer. Hastily she backed the horse under a spreading bush and held its nostrils so that it shouldn't whinny and alert whoever was out there looking for her. She held her own breath as the sounds appeared to be all around her.

Then, incredibly, she was looking into Luke da Souza's eyes. He was holding back the branches and staring down at her.

'Hell, girl, you take some tracking! Why didn't you stop that mad rush when you saw us coming up behind you?'

She clung on to the horse, suddenly weak with relief. Her chest rose and fell as she gasped for air, feeling faint.

He caught her as she sagged.

'Hell's teeth! You're all in!'

'I . . . I thought you were some of Jackson's men coming after me,' she murmured weakly. She clung to him.

'Yes, well, the bastards aren't so far behind. They know which way you're heading and I reckon they'll be aiming to cut you off up the river. I've got Jonas and Ferengo with me and they know the country. If it wasn't for them, I'd have beeen looking for you like a needle in a haystack.'

Suddenly Ferengo was there with

them, grimfaced and looking more Indian than Mexican.

'We'll have to get moving. Jonas found us a place to fort up.' After giving Marie-Anne an encouraging smile, he moved off and they followed.

'Can you walk a bit further?'

'I can manage.'

'I'll take your horse. Just follow Ferengo.'

They moved about a quarter-mile upriver and came to overhanging rocks before a bend in the river itself. Here, there was mad rushing water that swirled and tossed and over long years carved out a smooth platform of rock. The current was strong and water lapped unceasingly causing a constant wearing away and so making a cave which, when the spring meltwater came down in torrents, was filled to overflowing. Now, it was a little haven that provided shelter during any summer storm.

Jonas had already broken trail so that the horses could be sheltered also.

There was no need to hide their tracks. Amos Jackson's men were no Indian trackers. Besides, the aim now was to repel raiders, dig in and do as they'd done in the army. Luke da Souza was now Major da Souza commanding his men.

He turned to Marie-Anne.

'Whatever happens, you're to remain here with the horses.'

'Yes, Luke.'

He smiled at her. 'Have courage. We'll get you out of here.' Then he was calling the two men. 'How much ammo have we got?'

'Enough to rout those bastards,' grunted Ferengo.

'Good. Now we'll spread out at three points. I'll take the higher ground and you two watch for them coming up the river trail.'

There was a short respite which da Souza used to advantage.

The three men worked hard, making several hides from rocks and dead wood from which they could fire and

145

roll away, giving the impression of a far greater number, a trick Major da Souza had used successfully during the war. Then they loaded up their guns and rifles and lay alert for any giveaway sound that would herald the men's stealthy approach.

Marie-Anne waited, shaking and terrified, with the horses in the over-hanging cave. The minutes ticked by and the horses fidgeted, hobbled by huge rocks. They smelled water and strained at their ropes to free themselves.

They took her attention away from the agony of waiting. She talked to them, stroked their flanks and calmed their twitching bodies, and in doing so, helped to calm herself.

She wouldn't allow herself to imagine what would happen to her if these three men were killed and she was left to the mercy of Jackson's mob.

Jonas was the first to detect the silent approach in the brush and his first shot and the scream that followed, signalled a sudden upsurge of men as they opened fire.

It was then the hides became useful as Luke and the half-breeds fired their rounds and rolled in the deep grass and came up shooting from all angles.

Jackson's men were bewildered. The quarry was only supposed to be three in number and the girl. Now it looked as if they'd run into an organized platoon. They fired at the plumes of smoke, exposing themselves as they did so, and the bullets that hit them came from another direction entirely.

The gorge echoed with the sharp whine and staccato sound of gunfire and, during a lull, Luke da Souza and his boys frantically loaded up again.

Luke now lay below Ferengo and Jonas but could wave to them and they to him. He smiled. It reminded him of the excitement during battle when the adrenalin was flowing and men did heroic deeds when drunk with the heady success of a battle well fought.

The enemy were faltering now. Luke

had counted six muffled screams and seen both Jonas and Ferengo bring down men who'd climbed up the ridge to get behind them. They'd taken a header into the river below which was now dangerously low because of the new dam.

If there had been a way across the river at this point it would have been easy to escape, but the sheer cliffs on the other side which made a huge backbone of rock running down into the Sweetwater Valley until the two rivers joined again, made crossing impossible.

As he crouched low, fired and rolled, his mind was working on what would be the next move. If he could get the girl away on to the other side of the river, Ferengo and Jonas could deliver her home and into the hands of the loyal villagers to be looked after while he went after Amos Jackson.

His aim was deadly and fast. He was getting impatient with these would-be killers who were proving to be under no real command and certainly slovenly in their aim. It was as if they had no real heart for the outcome. It proved Amos Jackson wasn't a popular boss.

Suddenly Ferengo and Jonas were both firing fast and not bothering to roll. Luke stood up and from his position could just see the retreating men. He counted eight men and two went down from shots from above.

He climbed up to where the half-breeds were positioned. They'd come together and were laughing as they took aim.

'It's like shooting jack-rabbits,' Ferengo grinned. 'I think they've had enough.'

Luke took a couple of quick shots at the scrambling men and missed, but caused enough dust to rise around them to make them dance.

'They'll go back to Jackson and tell him they ran into an army,' grinned Jonas. 'I suppose it was the army that taught you that trick about the hides?' Ferengo asked curiously.

Luke shrugged.

'It's been done many times from where I come from. Yes, we used them successfully during the campaigns, but actually they were first used by the mountain men and then the outlaws.'

'Well, they certainly work. Now what do we do?'

'We'll eat and then we'll push on upriver until we can find a way to cross to the other fork. If Jackson has any foresight he might just have a party waiting for us. We'll go slow, Indian style, and feel our way. Right?'

'And then, boss?'

'You two take Miss Marie-Anne back to your village while I go and visit Amos Jackson.'

'Shouldn't one of us come with you?'

'Nope! You've done your bit in coming after the girl. From now on it's my fight. I want it that way.'

The brothers looked at each other. They disapproved but still, orders were orders.

Marie-Anne heard them scrambling down to the cave. For a moment she held her breath, wondering . . . and then let it out in a sigh of relief when she saw Luke enter the cave.

'What's happened? Have they gone?' She could hardly speak.

'I told you everything would be all right.' Suddenly she was in his arms, crying noisily as she let out all the tension and terror. 'There now,' he said uncomfortably, and patted her back. 'You have a good cry while we brew coffee and dig up some food. You'll feel better when you're fed.'

But she wouldn't allow them to do all the domestic chores. She mopped her eyes and hiccuped, then went to the water's edge and scooped up water into her hands and dashed it into her face. She came back with her chin up and a weak smile.

'I'm all right now. What do you want me to do?'

After the hasty meal, they moved on, finding a trail that turned and twisted along the riverbank. Long ago it must have been used both by Indians and animals, but now it was choked and overgrown in parts, as if long forgotten.

Ferengo went ahead and scouted around, but there was no sign of movement and Luke became impatient to reach the crossing point.

It was then disaster struck.

They were moving single file down to the water's edge not far from the dam. It was an ideal spot now that the water level had fallen. A tidemark of rotted vegetation and dead wood marked the level at its highest and exposed holes made by water rats and other creatures. The level had gone down by more than three feet and it was still sinking.

They looked at it and Ferengo grinned. 'That'll sicken old Jackson when he gets a taste of what he dished out to the other settlers.' Then Ferengo coughed, looked bewildered and fell off his horse. Then came the report of a gun.

Luke took one look at Ferengo sprawled on his back and saw the spreading blood of a bullet wound. He twisted round to look for the enemy just as a whirling lariat dropped over his shoulders before it was pulling tight.

He just had time to slap Marie-Anne's horse on the rump before he was pulled from his own.

'The river! Jump!' Jonas gave him a startled look and, grabbing Marie-Anne's reins, raked his horse. The two animals galloped neck and neck for the river. Marie-Anne screamed as the plunge hurtled them into the centre of the swirling river and the current sent them downstream, the horses kicking out strongly.

The water was low, but in the centre there was still a channel deeper than the rest. It covered riders and horses nearly to the horses' shoulders. Luke's last sight of Jonas and Marie-Anne were their bobbing heads as they swept around a bend in the river.

Then he was being dragged over

rough ground by a horseman who seemed to delight in trailing him over cactus and tough brush.

He was scratched and bleeding when finally he came to rest before old Amos who was standing high on a boulder. He was grinning triumphantly.

'So I've got you at last! The man who killed my son. I could kill you right now but that's not what I want. I want you to suffer!'

Luke gazed up at him.

'What about my brother? You had him killed.'

Amos shrugged. 'I don't care a damn about your brother. For me, there's only Abe.'

'He was a traitor and you know it! And you were the one controlling him.' Amos started and Luke smiled. 'Oh, it was known. If the war hadn't collapsed when it did, you wouldn't be alive today! *You* were responsible for the killing of your son!'

'That's a lie! It's all lies! We were working for the good of the nation.

Civil War is no good for any country. It was right to try and bring it to a close! And we succeeded!'

'You've got a twisted mind! You didn't consider that you were throwing away men's lives. That your son's spying, by which you benefited, sacrificed numberless men? Your son was lucky. He died cleanly and quickly, not like some of the Confederate soldiers who were hounded night and day in muddy trenches, then shot in the back and left to die where they dropped without food and water or any kind of help!' Luke's hard tones were contemptuous.

'Enough! I don't want to hear any more!'

'No, because you can't bear to hear the truth! You prospered while we fought. That is why you own half of the Sweetwater Valley today! How many pieces of silver did it take?'

'God damn you, da Souza!' He nodded to the man who was pulling the rope taut. 'Bind him tight and throw him over his horse. God help you if he gets away!'

The cowhand grinned as he dragged in the rope until Luke was in danger of being trampled by the man's dancing horse. He was savagely trussed like a turkey ready for the spit and bundled roughly aboard his mount, the breath punched out of him.

Then came the long trek back along the river and up the slopes towards the eyrie which was the Jackson ranch.

Once during the journey, Amos came and clutched Luke's hair, dragging back his head so that they were eyeball to eyeball.

'I suppose I have you to thank for changing the watercourse? I'll deal with that later, but for now I'll spit in your face!' It caught Luke in the mouth. Then Amos dropped his head viciously so that it pressed into the horse's ribs and he was again staring down at the ground, his lips tight together.

Hate burned in him, swelled, rolled and roiled. He would endure anything that the crazy bastard could throw at him but in the end he would kill him. It would be like putting down a rabid dog.

At last his ropes were cut and he flopped down on to the ground and suffered the first pangs of pain as the numbed circulation in his ankles and legs returned. He was hauled upright and dragged inside the ranch house then flung down on the plank floor.

Hazily he could see Ned Jackson looking down at him and then felt a kick in the ribs as Amos said softly, 'Now show us just how much of a man you are and get up.' Luke gritted his teeth and willed his legs to support him as he struggled on to his knees to finally stand erect. He swayed like a drunken man.

'Now, Ned, rope his wrists and haul him up to the beams yonder, a wrist to each hook.'

Ned licked his lips. 'What you mean to do with him, Pa?'

'You mean what do *WE* mean to do with him. We'll start with whipping him. It'll be a pleasure to see him squirm.'

'Pa, I don't think we should do this thing.' Ned looked at his father with as much courage as he could muster.

Amos spat on the floor.

'You're a snivelling bastard!' Then he turned to Luke. 'Why the hell didn't you kill him instead of Abe?'

'Because Abe was the dangerous one. Ned only got shot because he sprang in front of Abe. Don't you know that Ned tried to save Abe's life?'

Amos turned to Ned. 'Is this true?'

Ned hung his head. 'Yes, goddammit! He was my brother, wasn't he, no matter what he was like. You might say that I did it on impulse. If I'd had time to think about it, I wouldn't have done it! Abe was a pig!'

Amos smashed him in the face and Ned went down, blood spouting from a split lip.

'You take that back, Ned, or I'll string you up with this bastard here! I'll have no bad mouthing your brother.

He was the only one of you with balls!'

Ned struggled to his feet. Several of the cowhands, hearing the brawl, crowded into the big room.

'You want some help, boss?' Art asked, looking at both Luke and Ned, curling his lips at the sight of the blood pouring from Ned.

'Yes, string both the bastards up to the rafters.'

'But what about Ned? He's only got one arm.'

Amos sighed. 'Use your head, dummy. Rig him up by his wrist and put a noose round his neck. That'll hold him.'

'But . . . but he's your only son!'

Amos breathed deeply. 'I haven't a son. Just do as you're told. I can't bear to look at him!'

Luke's strength was returning. He'd listened, astonished by the venom Amos held for Ned. He remembered Ned as a willing soldier during the last campaign. He'd reacted quickly to orders and his courage could not be faulted. It was only when Abe Jackson joined the three brothers in the same platoon that things had started to go wrong, the younger brothers clearly under the influence of their wilder brother.

Now, Luke felt great sympathy for Ned. He and his brothers must have endured a miserable childhood under the yoke of a tyrannical father.

'Cut him down,' he said sharply to Amos. 'He's not worth expending your energy on him. I expect you'll be doing the whipping yourself? Then why don't you enjoy yourself cutting me up?'

Amos walked up and down before them both. He saw Luke's defiance and he saw Ned's tears and they made him feel sick. The little bastard was yellow compared to this Confederate exmajor and, deep down, he admired the man as much as he hated him. If only Abe had been like him!

It was the first time Amos had ever criticized Abe to himself and faced the

160

fact that Abe wasn't perfect.

He looked at Ned again and then nodded to Art.

'Cut the bastard down and throw him out, and if he's still on my land in twenty-four hours, he's to be shot on sight!'

Art cut him down and bundled him outside.

'I'm sorry, Ned. You heard what your pa said. You'd better git before your old man changes his mind and we use you for target practice.'

Ned gave him a burning look. 'I'll be back!' he said and stumbled away.

Inside the ranch house, Amos Jackson poured himself a stiff whiskey and drank it neat in one gulp and then poured another, all the while staring at Luke and the way Luke's muscles strained and stretched as he hung, barely touching the floor, his wrists wide apart hanging from the hooks in the rough wooden beam.

He watched the perspiration run down into Luke's eyes.

'When are you going to start begging, da Souza?'

Luke lifted his drooping head with difficulty.

'Go jack yourself!' His head dropped.

Jackson stormed forward and jerked Luke's head up and peered into his face. Luke smelled the whiskey breath.

'You cost me my family, da Souza! If it wasn't for you . . . ' He let Luke's head drop, emptied his glass and tossed it violently into the fireplace. 'God damn you, da Souza!' Taking down the bull-whip that hung coiled on a hook on the wall, he proceeded to hack several yards from it, until he had a whip that could be used in a confined space. Then he flexed what was left through his fingers feeling the hard knots of metal woven into the plaited thongs. He licked his lips.

'This is going to give me the greatest pleasure.'

Big Art watched from the doorway as the first swish of the thong curled about Luke da Souza's back. Then he closed the door and stood with his back to it and faced the bunch of men who stood in front of the ranch.

'I think we're going to have a long wait, boys.'

7

Although the river was much lower now, it still flowed swiftly in the centre channel. The dam itself, hastily built, still allowed much water through. But it was the dam that saved Jonas's and Marie-Anne's lives. She'd screamed and clung to her horse's neck as it plunged into the water, and gasped heaving breaths as the cold hit her. Jonas struggled to hang on to the reins of her mount, but was having trouble with his own young horse which had only forded shallow water and was fighting the current, bobbing up and down in a frenzy.

He cursed and jerked the horse's head upwards and it seemed to find a rhythm in the kicking of its forelegs. Then Jonas gave his attention to Marie-Anne.

'You all right?' he shouted, against

the roar of the water.

She gasped and nodded, not hearing his words but understanding his meaning.

'Hang on! I've seen a shelf of rock on the other side. If we can reach it we might find a way through the cliff. If not . . . ' He didn't finish for he knew that if they missed that vital point then they would be swept right through the gorge, the cliffs on the other side rising perpendicularly as if Snake River had cut through the rock like a wire through cheese.

'It's cold . . . ' Marie-Anne's teeth chattered and her hands were numb. 'I . . . I don't know how long I can hold on.'

He looked at her helplessly, seeing the white face turning blue and her clawing hands that were like talons.

'Pull on your left rein. Drag his head to the left . . . to the left! Go on, girl, you can do it. We've got to get to the other side!' He dragged on both horses' reins until they were heading gradually into more shallow water. Then the horses trod water. When they became aware of the sandy bed of the river, they gave great plunging leaps and, with a shower of water, strained their haunches and scrambled out on to the lip of black granite and stood trembling.

Jonas dismounted in seconds and lifted Marie-Anne tenderly off her mount. She was shivering, her limbs rigid and uncontrollable. He laid her down but had nothing to wrap her in. It looked likely that although they were saved from drowning, they both might die of cold.

He hobbled the horses and explored the crevice of rock behind them. It was a fault, a mighty cracking of rock during the Ice Age. It must lead somewhere, if they were lucky. If not, they would have to abandon the horses and climb the sheer cliffs. He might succeed, but he doubted whether Marie-Anne could.

The opening was wide enough for

the horses to get through. He took heart. There were lots of mountain passes sculpted by water and if this was an ancient dried-up waterway, then it would lead somewhere.

The darkness was total. He felt his way by touching the smooth walls on both sides. The ground beneath his feet was sandy so he'd guessed right. Smooth walls and smooth ground denoted a wearing away of stone by water over aeons of time.

He took heart. The air smelled fresh and he could walk upright and now and again the crack widened, but did not narrow to the extent he couldn't walk any further. Should he risk bringing in the girl and the horses?

He thought of the alternative and he knew he had no choice. He went back and found her comatose. He couldn't even light a fire to dry her clothes and his own condition worried him. They must keep on the move to keep the blood flowing.

He shook her and her eyes flickered

and opened and then realization hit her.

'You've got to get up and walk!' he said roughly.

'I can't. I just want to sleep!'

He shook her again.

'You can't sleep. If you do, you won't wake up!' He dragged her upright. Her legs gave way and he caught her as she began to sink down.

'You've got to fight it!' he bawled in her ear. 'God damn you, Marie-Anne, I thought you had guts!' Her head came up and for a moment fury showed in her eyes. Then the look faded and she was once more dazed and droopy.

He worked like a madman, lashing her wrist to her horse so she couldn't fall over. Then, walking by his own horse's side, he took her reins and forced both horses into the darkness.

He moved ahead and the horses followed. Every few yards, Jonas stopped and went back to see how Marie-Anne faired. She was still walking, although she didn't react when Jonas

168

touched her. She was walking like an automaton. At least, Jonas comforted himself, she was still putting one leg in front of another.

It seemed hours that they were slowly feeling their way through the great crevice and the ground now seemed to rise under their feet. Jonas was sweating, his clothes half dried. He could smell the river on him.

It had been some time since he'd checked on Marie-Anne.

'You all right back there?' He daren't stop for he was so tired he might not whip his body into moving again.

'Yes,' came the muffled reply. 'Where are we?'

'I don't know, but the darkness doesn't seem so black. Maybe we're coming to some kind of outlet.'

'There seems to be a draught.'

'Yes, the air's fresh. It's getting colder. Can you keep walking?'

'I'm managing. My wrist's sore because of the rope. The pain's keeping me awake.'

'Good. You're a gutsy girl, Marie-Anne.'

'You said I had no guts.'

'That was to make you angry.'

'It did, and I don't think I'll ever forgive you!' Jonas smiled into the darkness.

'That's John Lacey's daughter talking. You hate me good, and we'll get out of this.'

'Jonas?'

'Yes, Marie-Anne?'

'You're a brave man. I'll never forget you for this.'

'Just you go on hating me, girl, and keep your backbone stiff. We can talk about what you really think of me when it's all over.'

'You think we'll get out?'

'Of course. We're not meant to die yet, or the river would have finished us.' He sounded sure and she was comforted but inwardly he was not sure at all.

Then suddenly both were aware of new smells, a mixture of animal

170

droppings, rotting meat and smoke. The darkness was turning grey.

Then Jonas was walking forward into the daylight followed by the other horse dragging Marie-Anne with it. The old man squatting by a small fire at the mouth of the cave, dropped the turkey leg he was gnawing on and stared as if he had seen ghosts. Then he was clambering to his feet, ready to run. He opened his mouth to cry out and Jonas's voice stopped him. He spoke in mountain Cheyenne.

'Stop! We are not spirits of the mountain. We are those whom the river spurned.' The old man's eyes were still wide with terror. He could not speak. His jaw worked but no sound came. Jonas feared that he would be struck down in a fit. He tried again. 'The squaw is balanced between life and death. Can you help her, old man?' Jonas was holding the sagging Marie-Anne and the old man's wits were returning. This was a real woman, who needed his help as so many women had done in days gone by.

'I am a shaman,' he mumbled. 'I can help.' He pointed to an evil-smelling bed made up of an ancient buffalo skin spread on balsam branches which now smelled musty. 'Lay her down and I shall look at her.'

Jonas watched him while he stooped over Marie-Anne. He was bowed of shoulder and shrunken and his once sinewy arms thin with age. His hair was long and grey and in two plaits. An old deer thong was knotted around his forehead holding a single eagle's feather, a little askew at the back of his head. He wore ancient leather chaps and worn moccasins and a highly decorated jerkin that had seen better days. Also around his neck, were several amulets hung on thin strips of deerskin.

'You live all alone, old man?' Jonas ventured as the old man examined the girl.

'Yes. I have come back to the land of my fathers to die. We lived in the

Sweetwater Valley many moons before the white men came. You are the first to come up the secret Snake stairway. Long years ago it was known as the ancient way to eternity; men and women who grieved or were beyond human help, made their way through the eternal darkness and never came back. You say the way leads to the river?'

'Yes. The river was not hungry for our flesh. We braved the eternal darkness and now we are here. You can save her?'

The old man nodded.

'If the spirits want her alive, she will live. Now you must strip her while I mix herbs with whiskey and I shall massage her all over until her blood sings again.' He moved away and searched through a miscellany of objects in an old Indian parfleche and produced a bottle of whiskey. He offered it to Jonas. 'Drink of it, my friend, and give her some, but don't waste it. I'll find the herbs I need.'

He also built up the fire with dead wood until it was crackling merrily and throwing out heat. Jonas's damp clothes began to steam.

He drank and felt the fire reflected in his belly. Then he propped up Marie-Anne's head and made her drink until she coughed. Then he got down to the delicate business of stripping Marie-Anne of her wet clothes. He averted his eyes whenever he could, but there were times when he had to look at her and he marvelled at her long slim beauty and the difference between her and his comfortably plump wife, Chica.

Then he stepped back as the old man poured whiskey into a bowl, added pungent herbs, garlic amongst them, and commenced to rub her down from head to foot. He covered her with an old blanket as he proceeded down her body and limbs.

Jonas saw the pink glow return to the milky-white skin and was satisfied. He busied himself putting Marie-Anne's clothes to dry around the fire.

Then when all was done, the old man lifted an iron pot on to a trivet that swung over the fire, and soon the rich aroma of stewed turkey tickled their nostrils. Jonas's stomach growled for lack of food.

There was only one bowl so Jonas fed the girl first. She ate greedily and seemed to gather strength at each bite. She'd stopped shivering and the smelly blanket helped to retain the heat that had been engendered through the Indian's ministrations.

She thanked him with a smile as Jonas ate. The old man's withered hand stroked the hair from her face.

'You will see many years before you enter the next life. You are here for a purpose. Perhaps you are to bring back happiness to the valley. It has long been haunted by white men's lusts. I see it again as the valley it was meant to be. You are part of its regeneration.'

She looked up at him. 'Who are you?'

He smiled down at her, his wrinkles

reminding her of a withered nut.

'I am He-who-sees-beyond-the-horizon, one time known as Fleet-as-the-deer, but now I am only known as Sage. You can call me any one of these.'

'I shall give you a new name. You are my Mountain Father.'

He bowed gravely.

'It is an honour, and what should I call you?'

'I am Marie-Anne Lacey. My father has . . . ' She stopped and bit her lip. 'Did have the ranch at the bottom of the valley.'

'Ah, your father was John Lacey, and you,' he said turning to Jonas, 'must live in the village close by?' Jonas nodded. 'Then you are part Cheyenne like myself.' He turned to Marie-Anne again. 'Your father was a good man. Many times he helped the mountain Cheyenne when times were bad and the spring was late and the snow stayed with us and we could not hunt. We honour him for that.' His old eyes gleamed. 'You say he is dead?'

Jonas saw the girl's tears and spoke for her.

'We have had much trouble in the valley. Amos Jackson who owns the big ranch has routed the small ranchers and fired the town and caused many deaths, John Lacey amongst them.'

'And is this thing still going on?'

'It is. We escaped him and his men by plunging into the Snake River. My brother was killed and, even now, one of our number is being held by him. God knows if he is still alive!'

'And what about the townsfolk? Do they not rise up and fight this ruthless man? Or have they the spirits of hyenas and run and squawk like cowards?'

'They need a leader, and the man to lead them is now a prisoner.'

'Then you must leave at once. Go and find help and attack an hour before dawn as we did in the old days. Fire his lodge and take no prisoners and clean out the rottenness that is in the valley.'

'But what about the girl?'

'She can stay here. I shall look after her.'

Jonas hesitated and looked at the girl. She was looking much better, her colour returning.

'You will be all right with Sage?'

She nodded urgently. 'He is right. You must go and get help.' Weary as he was, he agreed, and they watched him mount his horse and ride away.

★ ★ ★

Amos Jackson watched the sagging body with satisfaction. The last three lashes across the shoulders had brought little response except for a convulsive shudder. He'd taught the bastard a lesson that no man could mess with the Jacksons, and this man more than any other.

His mind was obsessed with keeping him alive but determined to prolong the suffering as long as humanly possible. Da Souza would pay over and over again for the death of Abe.

He threw a bucket of water over him. Luke jerked and gasped and his eyes opened. He laughed in Amos's face.

'Thanks, I needed that,' he gritted, and fell silent again, concentrating on blanking out the pain of his lacerated back.

Suddenly the back door from the cookhouse opened and Ned stood in the doorway.

'Pa, you can't do this! He was only doing his duty!'

Jackson turned swiftly to face him.

'How did you get in? I told you to go!' he snarled. It was then that Luke drew up his legs and struck out with all his remaining strength and kicked the old man in the throat. Amos staggered back a couple of steps and then slammed into the wall, the whip jerking from his hand and snaking across the floor.

Ned stared at his unconscious father and then at Luke.

'For God's sake untie me!' Luke said.

Ned, with another fearful glance at his father, moved forward and with two cuts loosened the wrist bonds holding Luke to the beam.

Already the old man was moving and groaning. A few more minutes and he'd yell and raise the alarm. Luke struggled to rise from the ground and Ned dragged at him with one hand.

'Pa will kill me when he knows what's happened,' he gasped in a panic.

'Help me. Get me out of here and come with me.'

Ned didn't hesitate. He gathered up Luke's guns and his own and supported Luke who put an arm about his shoulder and they staggered into the cookhouse and out of the ranch house and into the backyard where the privy and a row of pigstys were built.

'Quick!' Luke urged. 'We'll hide in the biggest pigsty.'

'What? Among the pig shit?' Ned turned down his mouth.

'What better place? They'll never look in the sties.'

They hunkered down with six piglets being fattened for pork. They squealed a little and scampered around the sty, but when Ned tipped a bucket of swill that was standing ready to be thrown into the trough they stood in line and ate greedily, ignoring the two men inside the little wooden building.

Then came the mighty roar from inside the ranch house. Luke could feel Ned shiver as he leant against him for support. Two men charged round the back of the ranch house with two wolfhounds on chains. They yelped and sniffed and scrabbled in the dust, but were balked by the pig smell. They moved off and Ned whispered hoarsely, 'I forgot about the hounds. We wouldn't have got far. They're trained to run down any quarry, man or beast.'

'We'll let 'em run themselves ragged and when all's quiet we'll make for the horses.' Then, Luke said softly, 'Why did you interfere? After all, I was the one who shot you.'

'I looked on it as an accident. If I hadn't been fool enough to try and save Abe you wouldn't have shot me.'

'And you bear no grudge because I killed him?'

Ned hesitated and then said bitterly, 'He was a bastard, like my father. It was always him and Pa against me and Mark and Hank. I've cursed myself many times for getting shot up because of a swine like him. If I'd had the guts I should have shot my father down. Instead, he's hunting us like animals.'

Luke grunted. The pain in his shoulders was excruciating and now that the oozing blood was crusting over, it was agony moving his back and arms. The remains of strips of cloth that had been his shirt, stuck to him. He knew he needed the wounds cleaning, especially now that he was plastered with pig muck.

'Listen out for the men saddling up to go looking for us and when they're gone, we'll go inside and face the old bastard.' Luke closed his eyes and leaned against the sodden plank wall.

There were shouts and yells as the men searched the granary and the stables below the hayloft. They mangled up the hay, stabbing at it with hayforks and tossed straw bales about in the barn, but there were no men hiding anywhere.

Art scratched his head. His heart wasn't in it. He looked at the boss.

'They're nowhere about, boss. Ned must have had horses saddled and they got away under cover of that there stand of trees,' he said, pointing in the direction of the cluster of pines.

'If that's so, then they're heading south to Lacey's ford. It's the only way they can cross over the river. You take the men and ride after them. I can't ride; the bastard caught me in the throat and my head's going round fit to bust.' His voice was hoarse.

'Very well, boss. D'you want someone to stay with you?'

'No. Get everyone out there looking for the creeping slimeballs! There'll be a bonus for the men who bring them in!'

Art perked up. Talk of bonuses made the hunt interesting. He'd keep quiet about the bonuses. No need to let the men know. He could pocket the lot himself.

Amos Jackson leaned against the veranda upright and watched his men thunder out of the yard and fan out as they covered as much ground as possible. The hunt was on.

They hunted all day, the dogs working the thickets, the men exploring draws, all frustrated because they couldn't find horse tracks on the hard ground. It was as if the two men had vanished into thin air. Little did they know of the drama taking place in the ranch itself.

Amos turned and stumped into the house, his throat throbbing from the violent kick he'd sustained. He sought the whiskey bottle and poured himself a stiff drink. The alcohol burned and numbed his throat. He poured another and sprawled on the settle by the dead fire, his eyes wandering to the bloodstained whip still lying where it had fallen.

His hands turned into white-knuckled fists when he thought of Ned and his betrayal.

I shouldn't have cut him down, he ranted to himself. I should have given him what I gave da Souza. Wherever he is, he can't have gotten far in his condition. The thought gnawed at him that he'd been tricked somehow. Ned was too stupid to know how to vanish like that but da Souza . . . that devil was capable of anything. Again came the reluctant admiration for the man. God! If he'd had four sons like da Souza, he could have conquered the world!

He heard a sound coming through the fog of whiskey. He listened, ears straining until they ached. Then, unaccountably, his heart quickened and he turned stiffly on the settle and looked towards the inner door.

'We meet again.'

Amos watched dry-mouthed as his son Ned appeared behind the man now supporting himself against the door jamb. He swallowed, his throat dry and burning. He saw his future in da Souza's eyes and turned helplessly to Ned and saw the same there.

'You can't do it! You can't kill your own father!' he managed to utter as he watched Ned's handgun point at his head.

'You always said that only Abe was your son. That we were our mother's bastards. There's nothing to stop me . . . ' It was then that Luke slapped a hard hand down on Ned's wrist and fired with his other hand.

Amos looked surprised and a tiny hole appeared between his eyes.

Luke glanced at Ned.

'I couldn't let you do it, boy. Whether he was or wasn't, it don't seem right that you should live with the consequences.'

Ned's pale face suffused with colour.

The relief that it was all over and that he didn't need screw himself up to the point when he could pull the trigger, drained what courage he had out of him.

He cried and Luke slapped his face hard.

'Snap out of it, boy. If you want to be of help, then clean my shoulders and give me a shirt. Then I'll be off.'

'And where do you think you're going in your state?'

'Have you forgotten? There's a girl out there somewhere, if she's still alive. I'm going to look for her.'

Ned gave him a long hard look.

'She means a lot to you?'

'You might say that. She and her pa saved my life. I owe her.'

Ned nodded. 'Then I'll patch you up and get a pack of food ready. You'd better take one of Pa's bottles of whiskey. You'll need it.'

The problem was, which way to go. Ride north towards the gorge where Jonas and Marie-Anne had made a bid for freedom, or south towards Lacey's ford? Luke figured that if they did get away, then they would be moving south. He'd make for Lacey's ford and work upriver from that side.

He rode all night, only stopping to drink from the river and eat some of Ned's supplies. Twice he swallowed some whiskey when he felt as if he would fall off the horse from fatigue. But he carried on, and it was an hour after dawn that he heard the gunshots. There was trouble ahead.

He rode up to a high point and, as the sun's rays came over the far mountains, he saw far down below puffs of smoke and heard the sound of gunfire on the breeze.

He watched and saw that the ford was being defended. Shots came from the far side of the river. Jackson's men were fanned out along and before the river itself. From his viewpoint he could see several still figures sprawled on the ground. He narrowed his eyes to focus on those who were attacking Jackson's men and preventing them from crossing the river. He watched for a long time and then suddenly glimpsed a moving figure and recognized Carlos, John Lacey's man.

So, the villagers were fighting back!

He looked about him. How could he, one man, help from this side? Then he saw the clusters of boulders, large and small, that dotted Amos Jackson's side of the valley. The land rose sharply and from where he stood he could see the whole valley in its beauty and, in the hollow, the river, which was divided and came back to merge together at the far end of the valley.

Could he possibly start a landslide? Prise one of those boulders loose so that its momentum would send others crashing down on to the men below? It was worth a try.

He tethered his horse on a grassy stretch and proceeded to climb. Every step tormented his back muscles and the weals across his shoulders started to bleed. He could feel the warm stickiness as he battled his way up.

He targeted a boulder taller than himself. It teetered on an edge of rock. It looked as if a push would send it rattling down to crash on others, but was stuck fast. He sweated and strained and then stopped to rest, his heart pounding.

Then he squatted and looked at the base and saw that the boulder was nestling on cracked shards of flint. He looked back up the rising slope and saw other outcrops.

Then he was wildly scrabbling around to find a flint shard he might use as a lever. Surely he could either gouge out some of the flint and rock the boulder, or he might dig beneath it!

It took a mighty effort to loosen up the exposed flint and drag pieces free. The edges were sharp and he suffered cuts to his hands. Finally, heaving and pushing, he felt the first tremor of the boulder. It was finally lifting itself from its resting place!

That first movement gave him

strength. It surged in him and he gritted his teeth and pushed until the sweat burst from his brow, running down his cheeks, and he could feel the sting of it running down his back.

The boulder rocked. Backwards and forwards, hardly perceptible and then a little more drunkenly, until at last its own weight sent it toppling, and Luke sank to his knees.

The noise of its passing was like the roll of distant thunder. Luke, lying panting on the ground, could hardly believe what was happening. The ground shook and other rocks not too deeply embedded in the flinty ground, shivered and strained and split from their resting places with the crack as of ice breaking. The rocks gathered momentum and tumbled and bounced until the whole of the land seemed to be shifting.

He could still hear the faint sound of gunfire from down below, but now the tempo changed. There were screams of terror and men on horseback suddenly appeared racing away in all directions.

The landslide was now in full flow and showing its terrible power. Nothing would stop it now and the sight awed Luke. It was a gash of loose shale and newly exposed rocks ending in a growing mound that threatened to spill into the river. The Jackson land would never be the same again.

Later, down below, he saw no signs of the dead men. They were now covered by a mass of shale and rock.

Luke's horse slithered and struggled, haunches tensed, as it picked its way through the loose shale down the steep slope. He could see riders already fording the river, tiny moving specks that grew larger as he made his way down.

He waved. There was an answering shout. When on firmer ground, he galloped towards the bunch of riders who were fast coming together.

Then Carlos and Jonas were galloping towards him, as the rest of the men fanned out looking for survivors or bodies.

'What the hell happened up there?' Jonas boomed, as they came together. 'Why, man, you're lucky to be alive!' Then he looked Luke over. 'You're covered in blood. What happened?'

Suddenly all the reserve energy flowed out of Luke and he sagged, dizzy and weary, and his head dropped to his chest. Carlos was off his horse in a flash and was just in time to catch Luke as he fell sideways from the saddle.

'Hell! The feller's all in,' he said, as he eased Luke to the ground. 'Give us your flask, Jonas, he needs a snort right fast.'

Both men squatted by Luke as he drank and choked on the fiery liquor. He sat up and shook his head to clear it.

'I'm all right. Just a little short on sleep. What happened down here?'

'We stopped Jackson's men from crossing over. We were waiting for them and took out three before they knew we'd hit 'em. We were causing merry hell, and bullets were flying both ways when the boulders began to roll. Jees! We thought at first it was the echoes of the guns that started the landslide, but it kept coming and we knew it was something else. Don't tell me you started it?'

Luke shrugged.

'That damned boulder was ready to topple. A ground tremor could have started it at any time. I just gave it a helping hand. But I'm not worried about what happened here, where's Marie-Anne? I guess you both got out of the river together?'

'She's safe,' grinned Jonas. 'She's way back up the gorge with an old shaman. She'll be glad to see you.'

'Thank God! I thought you might both have been swept away.'

Jonas looked grave. 'It was touch and go with the girl. The old Indian saved her life. Massaged and pummelled the life back into her. I've seen nothing like that old feller. Knew exactly what to do for a half-frozen body.'

'And he's looking after her?'

'Yeah, I left her behind so's I could travel fast and gather up some of the townsfolk and the villagers to settle Jackson's hash once and for all.'

'Jackson's dead!'

Jonas stared at him. 'You killed him?'

'Yeah, it was either me or Ned. He's a good guy is Ned. You'll all fare better with Ned as boss from now on. He was going to kill his pa, but I stepped in and did it for him.'

Jonas nodded. 'I reckon you did right. No man should kill his own pa.'

'Anywhere I can kip down and get some sleep? I mean to start at dawn and go find Marie-Anne.'

'You need that back of yours cleaning. I'll take you to my wife, she's an expert. When dawn comes, I'll ride along with you and show you the way.'

Dawn came too soon for Luke. He

yawned and struggled awake. It seemed a long time since he'd slept under a roof. He thanked Cara for the food and attention and he, Jonas and Carlos rode away. They followed the river and saw how much higher it was since the new dam had been built. Jonas grinned.

'Soon it will overflow and we'll have grass and the crops will grow and this side of the valley will become green again as it used to be.'

They came to the merging of the two rivers into one and paused on an outcrop of rock to watch the trickle of water now coming down from Jackson's side of the valley.

Carlos frowned at the sight.

'It don't seem right. It's all out of balance. Not like it used to be. Man shouldn't try and change nature. There's always a price to pay. Look how our side of the valley withered and died.'

Luke nodded. 'It's easy enough to put right. We can tear down the dam.

It was built; it can be torn down.'

Jonas groaned.

'It's a hell of a long way to reach it. Maybe Ned Jackson will send men to tear it down.'

'Always supposing Amos's men will rally round Ned. Some of them might have left the valley.'

'Yeah, those not buried under that slide,' Carlos said morosely.

They rode on, all busy with their own thoughts.

They passed the devastation that was now Sweetwater Butte. Blackened and charred beams remained of wooden houses. The main store was gutted as was the hostelry. A blacksmith's anvil lay drunkenly amidst a mass of charcoal. Already makeshift tents straggled along what had been Main Street as the townsfolk searched amongst the debris for anything useful.

The smell of smoke still hung over everything. The blacksmith came to meet them accompanied by the barber and the undertaker. The three men drew rein. It was obvious the men wanted to talk.

'You be the man from Socorro, that John Lacey sent for?' said the blacksmith.

Luke nodded. 'Yeah, sorry I wasn't of more help.' He looked about him. 'There's a lot of work and organizing to do around here.'

'Will you stay and help?'

Luke pushed his hat to the back of his head and considered.

'I might, if conditions were right.'

'We'd pay. We never needed a sheriff or a mayor before. We was law-abiding and helped one another until it all changed and Jackson rode rough-shod over us.'

'You can be that way again. It only takes organizing.'

'That's what we want, an organizer who can get things done. We think you as an army major will fit the bill. You'll stay?'

'As I said, maybe, if conditions are right.'

'Do you *have* to go back to Socorro?'

'Nope. I have no ties there. Just working on a cattle ranch. I'll not be missed.'

'Then why not give us your answer?'

Luke took a deep breath.

'I'll tell you when I'm good and ready. Now, we're on our way to bring Miss Marie-Anne home to her ranch.'

'Ah, that's it, is it? You're waiting to see what future you have with the girl!'

Luke glared at the blacksmith. 'Mind your own business, big man! Come on, boys, let's be on our way.'

They travelled on and occasionally Jonas glanced at him.

'It's true what Jake said, isn't it? You're sweet on Marie-Anne?'

'What's it to you?'

Jonas shrugged. 'She's a nice girl. I'd like to see her fixed up, especially now her pa's gone, and she couldn't do better than take you. She's the prettiest girl in the valley.'

Luke grunted. 'That's just it. She might think I'm only after the ranch.'

He looked broodingly ahead as they rode. 'She's only a kid. She should have her chance to meet others.'

Jonas laughed. 'And leave her wide open to other chancers? Besides, she's a strong-minded female and might have ideas of her own. She was mighty glad to see you again.'

'That means nothing. She and her pa saved my life. I suppose she was glad for all the nursing they did.'

'Aw, to hell! As a major with military experience you can't be beat; as a man with a woman, well . . . I could beat you hands down!' Jonas grinned as if at a private joke.

They set a gruelling pace and soon, after the ground started to rise and they were in the foothills, the terrain became dull and grim and much colder. Also they heard thunder in the far distance rolling around the mountain tops.

'Sounds like a change of weather,' Carlos grunted, and didn't sound too pleased at the prospect. 'We're going to get an early rainy season.'

'Good for the grass and the farmers and their crops,' muttered Jonas.

Luke barely heard their utterances. He was deep in thought about Marie-Anne.

At last they found themselves on the high ridge of rock running alongside the Snake River and Jonas pointed out the old Indian's cooking fire. The smoke rose lazily in the air.

But now the thunder seemed nearer, and there were sharp flashes of lightning. They hurried to get undercover before the rain came down.

Sage grinned when he saw the three men leading their horses for the last few yards and Marie-Anne flew outside the cave and flung herself into Luke's arms.

'You got away from that awful man! I've been so worried about you!' She hugged him, making him flush, as Jonas grinned openly to Carlos as if to say I told you so. 'Of course I've been worried about you too, Jonas,' Marie-Anne finished, a little guiltily,

201

but giving Luke another hug, thereby making him cringe as she pressed on his shoulders.

Then, her eyes big and round she examined him and let out a scream.

'Sage! Look at him! I don't know how he's been able to ride all the way here!' Sage looked and tut-tutted and went looking for bear fat and a concoction of pine needles to soften the scabs and disinfect any likely infection.

While he was being doctored by Sage, the thunder crashed overhead and the rain came down in a sudden heavy downpour. The noise was so hard they couldn't hear themselves speak.

Carlos got fidgety as the lightning flashed and one thunder roll after another rent the air. There was the smell of sulphur. Water ran down the rocks and soon there were tumbling rivulets of water, all making their way down to the river.

Carlos stood at the opening and looked out at the vista of hills and valley and then he turned sharply to face the others.

'I don't like it. It's getting worse.'

'What's it matter, Carlos? We're high and dry here in this cave.'

'You don't understand,' Carlos burst out, 'it's the dam.'

'What about it?' Luke asked, putting on his shirt.

'What dam?' Sage looked puzzled.

'The dam above the fork,' answered Carlos. 'It's stopping the flow down the other side of the ridge. All the water is going down one side.'

'Well, that's what you wanted, isn't it?' asked Luke comfortably. 'You were against Jackson damming your side. Now you've got all the water you want.'

The Indian let out a mighty wail. Then he was leaping up and down and hollering as if chasing evil spirits from the cave.

'What in hell . . . ?' gasped Luke.

Then Sage was before them and now he was shaking.

'You say there is a dam? Then it must come down, or the water will spread over the valley. Once, many years ago when I was a boy, there was a beaver dam up there and it covered one of the forks. When the rainy season came, the Indian village down below was drowned and everyone with it. The water comes suddenly. That is why we never allowed the beavers to breed up there. The white man's interference is too much! It must come down!'

The men looked at each other, awed and worried.

Jonas said what they were all thinking. 'We can't go out in this weather!'

But Carlos sided with Sage.

'Whether we like it or not, it must be done. I've been uneasy about the dam ever since I knew it was rebuilt on our side. I'll go alone if I have to!' He poured coffee for himself, and stuffed some bread and meat into his mouth and was ready to go.

Sage followed, muttering about all hands needed. The others came after.

They rode with heads down through the blinding rain that hit them like icy needles. Now they were riding by the river which was a tumbling whitewater and already bursting its banks in parts.

They all knew it was the most dangerous task they would ever do in their lives. But Sage had a surprise for them when finally they arrived and stood high over the tumbling water, looking down from slippery wet rock.

'How the hell do we tackle that?' shouted Jonas, as they inspected the makeshift dam. Already the brushwood was loosened, but the heavy boulders and rocks were still standing fast. 'We'll be washed away in the flood!'

Now Sage was grinning, and he pulled from under his blanket a bundle done up in oilskin.

'What you got there, Sage?' Jonas asked.

'Dynamite!'

'Dynamite? How the hell did you get that?'

'It's loot I got from a goldminer. It's old but I suppose it will still go poof!'

Luke took it from Sage and carefully unwrapped it. He was an expert on explosives. He found six sticks all taped together. Enough to blow a dozen dams! He made his mind up quick. He would do the job himself without the help of the others.

He outlined his plan and they stared down into the rushing water, Sage shaking his head and muttering about mad white men, while Jonas insisted he should come with him.

'You can't climb down this wet rock all by yourself. One slip and you'd be washed away! No, you will need a rope . . . '

'And drag you down, too? No sir! It can be done. Besides, there's no telling how fast she'll blow in this weather. If I go alone, then I have only myself to worry about.'

He was adamant. There would be no one else with him. He could then gauge how much time he had and take cover. That was the plan and that was how it would be. No discussion!

He tucked dynamite and Jonas's supply of lucifers inside his leather jerkin and moved out into the storm. The rain came down like hammer blows intent on driving him into the ground. It was hard to breathe as the wind was rising. Carefully he crept to the edge of the cliff and a sudden flash of lightning showed up the black wet rocks and the swirling white water.

For a moment he felt dizzy as if carried away by the rush of water. Then he steeled himself and took his first tentative step and, gripping any foliage that had taken root between the rocks, he felt around cautiously for the next foothold.

The others huddled above watching each exploratory step, gasping when Luke's foot slipped or when he couldn't find a good hold on the slimy rock.

He was halfway down when he heard

a scream and saw a distraught Marie-Anne being held back by Jonas. He leaned against the rock to get his breath before cursing and roaring for them to take her away. She struggled against Jonas and it took both the Indian and Carlos to drag her away weeping.

'Sage, take her away! She's no business to be here! Knock her out if you have to, but for God's sake keep her away. God knows how the dam will blow when she goes, and that goes for all of you!' He didn't wait to see if they had heard him but went on, one foot at a time, until at last he was as near the edge of the river as possible and easing himself along to the nearest point he could get to the dam.

Far ahead he could see where the river divided. No one could calculate exactly what would happen when the water pressure and the watercourse was violently diverted. There was a devilish price to pay for interfering with nature.

He huddled in some semblance of

shelter as he fumbled for the dynamite. His hands were clumsy from the cold, his body sodden, and yet tension sent his blood pumping crazily. His mind was cool. He'd worked under pressure when his very life was at stake all through the war. He could do it now.

Quickly he gauged his throw against the wind, the distance involved and exactly where would be the best place to aim for. Yes, he would only get one chance. It had to be right.

He took a deep breath and, turning with his head against the rock, he lit the fuses, and watched while they spat and sizzled. He counted, coolly and deliberately, and then whirled and with outstretched arm, sent the smoking, sparking mass high into the air and watched as it turned over on itself and down.

He saw it reach its target and he scrambled away and threw himself under a small overhang of rock and prayed, with hands over his ears.

He waited, and for long seconds he

thought he'd missed the target and the dynamite had hit the water. He began to crawl out of his hole when suddenly the ground shook and a dull roar filled his ear. It was as if a mighty bore had come rushing down the river. The water rose and fell with dramatic suddenness. He felt it suck at him as the first pressure lifted and then he was lying in the wash of surplus water that was being rapidly drained into the other fork.

There came a faint cheer from above and he crawled out of his hole battered and gasping and waved to them above.

It was a success.

He leaned against the rock, rainwater washing down his face and watched as the volume of water balanced itself as it raced along the two water-courses. At least the valley floor would not now be submerged.

He felt strangely weak. He wanted to go with the flow. It mesmerized him. It was a long time before Jonas appeared beside him, shaken but determined.

'Are you all right? I've brought a rope. You look as if you need it.'

Luke didn't answer, but put an arm about him and Jonas tied Sage's old buckskin lariat about his waist and signalled to the others to hold it firmly.

Luke never did clearly remember that climb. All he could remember was Marie-Anne, sodden, long hair wet about her shoulders, holding him close and crying, and the ride back to Sage's cave and Sage massaging him with whiskey and some devilish herbal essence that smelled like forest trees but which made his body glow.

Then, much later when the rains had stopped and he felt like a man again, and he was back at the Lacey ranch, there was a deputation come to see him from the tented town of Sweetwater Butte asking whether he'd made a decision to stay.

He never could remember whether he'd ever actually made that decision, for a smiling Marie-Anne took over the meeting and answered all his questions for him. She was a very capable girl and she knew all the answers.

Yes, he was staying and yes, he would act as sheriff and mayor, and yes, he would be living here at the Lacey place and yes, and now she looked a little coy, they were going to be married as soon as possible. He needed someone to look after him, as he always had done.

Then she'd looked at him and laughed and hugged him. The townsfolk went away happy that they now had a leader, but all of them were glad their own womenfolk weren't *quite* so bossy!

THE END

Other titles in the Linford Western Library

THE CROOKED SHERIFF
John Dyson

Black Pete Bowen quit Texas with a burning hatred of men who try to take the law into their own hands. But he discovers that things aren't much different in the silver mountains of Arizona.

THEY'LL HANG BILLY FOR SURE:
Larry & Stretch
Marshall Grover

Billy Reese, the West's most notorious desperado, was to stand trial. From all compass points came the curious and the greedy, the riff-raff of the frontier. Suddenly, a crazed killer was on the loose — but the Texas Trouble-Shooters were there, girding their loins for action.

RIDERS OF RIFLE RANGE
Wade Hamilton

Veterinarian Jeff Jones did not like open warfare — but it was there on Scrub Pine grass. When he diagnosed a sick bull on the Endicott ranch as having the contagious blackleg disease, he got involved in the warfare — whether he liked it or not!

BEAR PAW
Nevada Carter

Austin Dailey traded two cows to a pair of Indians for a bay horse, which subsequently disappeared. Tracks led to a secret hideout of fugitive Indians — and cattle thieves. Indians and stockmen co-operated against the rustlers. But it was Pale Woman who acted as interpreter between her people and the rangemen.

THE WEST WITCH
Lance Howard

Detective Quinton Hilcrest journeys west, seeking the Black Hood Bandits' lost fortune. Within hours of arriving in Hags Bend, he is fighting for his life, ensnared with a beautiful outcast the town claims is a witch! Can he save the young woman from the angry mob?

GUNS OF THE PONY EXPRESS
T. M. Dolan

Rich Zennor joined the Pony Express venture at the start, as second-in-command to tough Denning Hartman. But Zennor had the problems of Hartman believing that they had crossed trails in the past, and the fact that he was strongly attached to Hartman's Indian girl, Conchita.

BLACK JO OF THE PECOS
Jeff Blaine

Nobody knew where Black Josephine Callard came from or whither she returned. Deputy U.S. Marshal Frank Haggard would have to exercise all his cunning and ability to stay alive before he could defeat her highly successful gang and solve the mystery.

RIDE FOR YOUR LIFE
Johnny Mack Bride

They rode west, hoping for a new start. Then they met another broken-down casualty of war, and he had a plan that might deliver them from despair. But the only men who would attempt it would be the truly brave — or the desperate. They were both.

THE NIGHTHAWK
Charles Burnham
While John Baxter sat looking at the ruin that arsonists had made of his log house, a stranger rode into the yard. Baxter and Walt Showalter partnered up and re-built the house. But when it was dynamited, they struck back — and all hell broke loose.

MAVERICK PREACHER
M. Duggan
Clay Purnell was hopeful that his posting to Capra would be peaceable enough. However, on his very first day in town he rode into trouble. Although loath to use his .45, Clay found he had little choice — and his likeness to a notorious bank robber didn't help either!

SIXGUN SHOWDOWN
Art Flynn

After years as a lawman elsewhere, Dan Herrick returned to his old Arizona stamping ground to find that nesters were being driven from their homesteads by ruthless ranchers. Before putting away his gun once and for all, Dan forced a bloody and decisive showdown.

RIDE LIKE THE DEVIL!
Sam Gort

Ben Trunch arrived back on the Big T only to find that land-grabbing was in progress. He confronted Luke Fletcher, saloon-keeper and town boss, with what was happening, and was immediately forced to ride for his life. But he got the chance to put it all right in the end.